DINOSAUR R

a fantasy inspired by the town of Seymour Arm, British Columbia and by my grandson, Austin.

C. H. DAVIDSON

iUniverse LLC
Bloomington

Dinosaur Rock
A fantasy inspired by the town of Seymour Arm, British Columbia and by my grandson, Austin.

iUniverse books may be ordered through booksellers or by contacting:

iUniverse LLC
1663 Liberty Drive
Bloomington, IN 47403
www.iuniverse.com
1-800-Authors (1-800-288-4677)

ISBN: 978-1-4759-1011-7 (sc)
ISBN: 978-1-4759-1012-4 (e)

Printed in the United States of America

iUniverse rev. date: 03/19/2014

CONTENTS

This Book is dedicated to:
—My grandson, Austin, who was the inspiration for the story.
—My geological friend, John Rivette who supported my work
throughout and offered much information
about the dinosaur world

The towns folk of Seymour Arm for their endless help and support

Many thanks to all of you.

Helena

CHAPTER ONE

Shadow Lake

"They're here!" I yelled, grabbing the last sausage from my breakfast plate. I ate it and wiped my fingers off on my shorts as I ran into the yard, Bessie, Grandpa's Bassett Hound, yapping at my heels. Ryan and Kayla piled out of the truck, rocketing straight toward me.

"How ya'doin', Austin?" Ryan said, punching my arm.

"Great," I said, punching him back, "Even better now that you guys are here."

"Hi Austin, when can we go to the beach?" Kayla said, stooping to pat Bessie.

"Let's go," I said, leading them to the bike shed. We took off, on our bikes, to the floating store. That's where the other kids would be gathering.

"Did you talk to Dr. G. about Saturday morning gardening?" Ryan asked, as we rode along.

"Yep, it's all set up same as last year, so we'll have spending money all summer."

"I'd rather be sorting dinosaur bones for him, he's got such a great collection from his working days as a paleontologist," said Ryan.

"Or polishing his rock collection." I added.

"Oh no," groaned Kayla, "here we go with the rock thing again."

"The bad news is that his 'golden grandson', Eric, is here for the summer too. He's got a purple, off center Mohawk this year and a brand new dirt bike. I think it's a present from his Grandpa," I said.

Both Kayla and Ryan groaned.

"Oh well, we're here and that's just great," said Kayla.

The air smelled of summer, even though the last of the spring flowers were still blooming. The gravel beneath my tires and the sun beating down on my bare back felt comforting. This was my Grandparents place, my summer place. Kayla, Ryan and I call it our second home. They're my cousins, and we've been spending our summers here since we were little kids.

"Let's hit the store before we go down to the beach, I want junk food," Kayla said.

"Yeah," I replied, "What's the beach without great eats?"

Walking our bikes up the steep hill, back from the store, I spotted the rock.

"Hey, dudes, look at this beauty," I shouted. Ryan and Kayla glanced at each other knowingly but they came over to my side of the road.

"Look at that rock shine!" I said.

"Not again," said Ryan, "you and your rocks,"

"It's just the mica causing it to shine, like all of the others," said Kayla.

"I know, but this one seems different to me." I picked it up; for a moment everything went fuzzy.

"Whoa, dizzy spell, too much sun already I guess," I said, "let's get to the water."

"We got onto the bikes and rode toward the beach. Coming around the corner near the Johnson cottage, we were nearly run off the road by Eric, on that motorcycle. I slid and the rock flew across the road as my bike fell. I got up and ran for the rock. Eric got their first and grabbed it.

He looked it over, then, suddenly tossed it back to me. Luckily I found it. I was overjoyed, and started to think about Bessie.

This rock isn't a pet! I told myself. *Why does it seem so important?*

"You geeks ought to watch where you're going." Eric yelled as he roared past.

I hardly noticed. I had started to feel dizzy again. "Let's go." I said, "I need to get into the water."

When we got to the beach, we parked our bikes and walked to the end of the dock. It's sort of a routine we have, to take a first look at the water together.

"Look," Kayla said, "That's what gives Shadow Lake its name."

We were looking at an odd quirk in the light that happens for a few minutes in the morning, most days. While the sun plays and glistens on the surface, the water beneath appears dark and fathoms deep. It's full of swaying shadows that speak of a vibrant, mysterious life. I know that it's just the mountains and clouds that cause it, but it still captivates me every time I see it.

The lake lies nestled in a long, low valley between tall, snow-capped mountains. It stretches for miles to the clear, blue horizon. Sparkling white sand rims the lake. A birch and pine tree forest stand silent and majestic, behind it, touching down to the shore in places and climbing high into the hills, until they stop and reveal the bare rocks above them. A wide, sandy path runs from the road to the beach. It ends at the dock, where we were standing.

"Look at that sand," said Kayla, "It's so sparkly, I wish I could bottle it up and take it home,"

"Personally, I like the water," grinned Ryan.

"Watch out for the dog," I yelled!

Too late. Bessie had run into the water, gotten soaking wet and then rolled in the sand. As soon as she got back to us, she shook like mad.

"Yuk, I've got sand everywhere," said Kayla. "Come here Bessie, let me tie you up."

Soon we had joined into a game of water volleyball. The splashing and laughing felt so good. After the game we had a swim and as I walked back into the shore, I noticed that it was just as weedy as last year though.

Why don't they clean it up, I thought.

We had a good day at the beach and I had forgotten about the rock entirely. It wasn't until bedtime that I remembered.

"Austin, shower time and I want your hair washed too," said Grandma.

"I'm really not dirty," I grumbled as I went into the bathroom.

Later, lying in bed, I noticed the rock, sitting where I had left it, on my dresser. I couldn't take my mind off it. Finally, I got up and put the rock under my pillow, cupping it in my hand. I felt a bit dizzy for a minute, but quickly fell asleep.

CHAPTER TWO

Dinosaurs!

I was standing on the top of a hill, over looking a lake. It was evening and waves were splashing against some rocks and slapping up onto the sandy beach in front of me

Where the heck am I?

I glanced down at the sand and my heart leapt into my throat! I saw giant, scaly, green claws! Shooting away at top speed, I tripped over my own feet and fell with a great thud. I rolled over, stood and ran in one motion but those green claws kept pace with my every move. The desperate roar of a wild animal near by scared me, but a quick glance behind showed me nothing. *I'm dead!!!* The roaring grew louder and more desperate. It seemed to be in my head, repeating and repeating until I felt swallowed up by it.

Blood raced through my veins. My body seemed impossibly weird and awkward. My stomach felt like a huge lump of ice and my hands felt icy and sweaty both at once.

Stay calm, Austin, just calm down. This is just a dream, you'll be fine.

Count to ten. One, two, three . . . ? What's next? What was I thinking about a minute ago? Why am I so upset? Oh yeah, I fell down, well so what? I looked around. *It's nice here.*

The air smelled fresh and sweet. I felt light headed, but also strong and full of energy.

I butted my head into a small tree beside me and it toppled over. Wow! I tried it a few more times, just for the fun of it, rutting at small trees and knocking them down. Incredible!

Swamp water lapped around my legs and felt warm and soothing. Tall, thick trees grew along side the small shrubbery and water-plants that were all around me. I reached out with my mouth and ate a few of the nearby leaves. They tasted fresh and juicy and sweet. I ate a couple more mouthfuls. Great stuff! I saw a river near by. I wandered over for a drink. The water lapped blue and clear right to the bottom. I drank. It was almost tasteless, but so refreshing. Then I saw it! Reflected in the water I could see an ugly green head with a long horn running straight back, from it's forehead to the back of its head.

What the heck? I started to back away slowly.

Its mouth was long and narrow and full of big, flat, dirty molars. Its front legs were short and skinny, but with gruesome claws. Its eyes seemed small, but somehow familiar. What was going on?

I backed down the shore a bit, until I could no longer see that sea creature. *What do I do now?*

I decided to run back into the forest. I sped away from the shore, into the trees. Gigantic bugs flew around me, landing on my face, my head, and my back. They didn't sting, I hardly even felt them. Flying lizards, or something like them, flew over head; cawing and grabbing at each other. Creepy all right, but I really didn't seem to mind them.

I tried to remember what I should be worried about, but I just couldn't. My brain seemed fogged over, and I just felt like wandering around. I started munching on the nearby leaves. The next second I heard a rumbling noise behind me and I turned to see what it was. A creature like the one I had seen reflected in the water roared and raced straight towards me! I ran and yelled for Mom as loud as I could. A horrible bellow scared me, even as I ran.

CHAPTER THREE

A Friend

The big creature overtook me in a flash and kept banging into my side, but gently, not hurting me. My mouth dry and my heart pounding, I slowed down a bit and glanced at him. *Ugly!* Tall and heavy with a long head and a horn right in the middle of it that sort of lay flat against his head, just like the one I had seen in the water. His legs, arms and claws seemed like that other ones too. His giant body was caked in mud and bugs that ate at the flakes of skin on his back. He looked to me like a dinosaur, but how was that possible? Why wasn't he hurting me? Was it me making that dreadful noise! Oh no!

I stopped running, and hardly daring to breathe, looked down at myself. *My feet, my legs! What's happened to me?*

Those green scales I'd seen earlier covered my whole body and my limbs. My hands had morphed into withered scaly claws. I felt the tears streaming down my face as I whispered,

"Mom, where are you? Grandma? Grandpa?"

The painful mew of a hurt animal echoed back at me. This time, I knew that I was hearing my own voice.

I look just like him, I thought, staring at the dinosaur creature beside me. Shock ran though me and I shuttered!! I knew that I was upset, but suddenly I couldn't remember why. I picked up speed and we ran side by side for a long way, then he started to slow down. Thank goodness! I was so tired! We walked along the beach for quite a way until he finally stopped for a drink in a wide creek that ran near by.

What a great idea, I gulped thankfully.

He didn't leave; he just stood near me and looked at me with his soft, small deep brown eyes. A scar ran across his nose making him seem kind of vulnerable.

He waded into the water, then turned and looked at me. He made a soft rumble in his throat, so I waded in too. We had a little swim and a roll in the mud on the shore. It felt cool and thick and slippery. My back stopped itching, and I realized that it had felt sore before. I still had the feeling that something was very wrong, but I kept forgetting what it was. I should be feeling good. I had just met up with a friend.

Wait a second! He's a dinosaur! I'm not a dinosaur, I'm a kid! Then that idea just evaporated.

I walked quietly beside him through the swamp. As we got to the other side, I saw a whole herd of dinosaurs that looked like my new friend, feeding on the nearby tree tops. My companion grumbled in his throat again and walked straight towards them. I followed cautiously behind him. Most of them didn't even notice when we joined the herd.

We ate silently for some time. Suddenly, I heard crashing noises and looked around. Everyone was running at full steam, bellowing loudly. The friendly dinosaur I had met pushed me ahead and then disappeared into the herd. I was shoved towards the middle. Again, I glanced behind me, and stopped dead still and stared. Fear prickled my skin. A sliver of icy cold blood chilled my veins.

A massive dinosaur roared in my face, showing grey/yellow teeth and a cavernous mouth. My heart thumped in my chest, as if about to explode. The monster reared and opened his toothy mouth as he caught up to one of the females and grabbed her hind leg. Blood spurted out everywhere. I turned and fled, running with the group, faster than I ever had before.

CHAPTER FOUR

Research

Austin, I heard faintly, in the back of my mind. It flashed away.

I kept running, not daring to look back. The thunder of hooves and the sad, desperate drone coming from my head, and all around me, kept me going even harder. I needed to escape from here, but how?

Austin, Austin, I heard again. White light flashed in front of me, but I kept running.

"Austin," I felt something grab my side and shake my body.

Then I saw a flash of light, and I was lying in my own bed, looking up at Ryan.

"What?" I mumbled, still half in the land of the dinosaurs and afraid of being eaten.

"Are you okay? You feel sweaty and hot, let me get a better look at you," Ryan said, reaching for the table lamp.

"No, its okay, I'm all right now; it was just a bad dream." I took his arm and moved it away from the lamp. "The light will wake me up too much, just let me go back to sleep, okay?" I rolled over and waited until I heard him walk away. I felt under my pillow for the rock.

It wasn't there. I found my flashlight and ran it around the room. The rock was lying on the floor. I got out of bed and picked it up. There was the dizzy feeling right away, it frightened me, so I threw the rock onto my dresser and climbed back into bed. I lay there a long time, thinking about the dream. It felt so real. Did it have something to do with the rock? Could something actually be happening to me when I held that thing in my hands? *Yeah, sure, like you change into a dinosaur! Not likely.* Still, I felt scared.

At breakfast, Ryan asked me how I was. I told him I was fine now, and that I appreciated him waking me up from my nightmare. He was still concerned.

"You were yelling loud enough for me to hear you from my bed across the room," he said, "and when I got there, you were thrashing around quite a lot."

"Thanks for checking on me, Ryan," I said, "sometimes I have nightmares, but I'm fine now." He left it at that.

After breakfast, when we were alone, I told Ryan and Kayla about the dream.

"It sounds like a really bad dream," said Kayla,

"Sorry about last night," I told Ryan, "I was too shook up to get into it then and I don't want Grandma and Grandpa to know about it," I said, "do you think there could be a connection between that rock I found and the dream."

"Right, like the rock is some magic route to one hundred million years ago," said Ryan, laughing, "don't be so crazy, Austin."

"But it seemed so real," I said. "I even knew what I looked like and felt like."

"I knew, last night, that something else was going on," Ryan said.

"Let's go on line and see if there ever was a dinosaur like the one you dreamt about."

A few minutes later we were in the computer world of dinosaurs. The dinosaur that I had dreamt about was a very common one, called a Hadrosaurus, one of the Duck Billed dinosaurs. He was a plant eater from the late Cretaceous Period. That was sixty to one hundred million years ago. He lived all over North America and was very common in the Shadow Lake area. We had known that the area had once been dinosaur country. There's a big museum about two hours from the lake and we had taken day trips there nearly every summer. I knew that I would recognize myself as soon as I saw a picture.

"I don't even know if my dream was about this area or somewhere else," I said. "I remember that there were big waves and the water was swampy, but it was likely that it was swampy way back then. I think this dinosaur is the right one, though, but it looks kind of funny in the pictures here. What I remember was being sort of fuzzy all over, and a tan color, not grays, and with a rougher hide."

"Well, that makes sense," said Ryan, "these are reconstructed from bones; how could they tell about stuff like skin and hair from that?"

"The front legs seem too short," I added, "but I guess that's a mistake they could make as well. Let's check out a few more sites."

After browsing through a lot of stuff, we got to know quite a bit about the Hadrosaurus. They roamed in great groups, called herds, all over the land. We also discovered that they protected their young until they were able to take care of themselves. Back then a lot more land was covered by ocean, but by the end of the Cretaceous Period, it was starting to dry up.

"Let's see if there's anything connecting dinosaurs directly to Shadow Lake," Ryan suggested.

We typed in both words and got more of the same info. Then Kayla came across a different type of page. It was a blog that read like a diary, and seemed to be written by someone who had discovered a dinosaur dig right here in Shadow Lake. It covered a few weeks of exploration and then ended.

"Well guys. Here's the last entry," she said, reading.

April 16th, 2007

> *Dinosaur bones at last, with help from my grandfather, who has been with me in the exploration, we now have a few good samples. I haven't told him yet about the cave, beside the dig site. I really don't know enough about it myself yet. I think about it all the time, though and I want to explore it more. I have never felt this close to the dinosaurs before. When I see*

them on the cave walls, I feel like I am almost right there with them.

Murray.

"I wonder what happened," said Kayla.

"And where the dig and cave are, and who knows about them now," added Ryan.

"And what's that about dinosaurs on the cave walls? I bet that Dr. G. could help us find out," I said.

CHAPTER FIVE

Dr. Gerard

We decided to ask Dr. Gerard about the blog we had found. When we got there, he answered our knock right away and welcomed us in.

He took us into his big, bright, cluttered living room and kitchen area. I've always liked it in this room. There's a fireplace between the living room and the kitchen and the fire can be seen from all around it. It's not lit in the summer, but it always warms me up anyway. There are rocks and gems displayed on every windowsill, inside and outside of the house, in every possible spot. I guess that's because he was a paleontologist before he retired.

I sat down over by the piano and noticed a photograph on it. I knew I had seen that face before, but I couldn't tell where.

"Dr. G." I asked, picking up the picture, "Who is this? He seems to be someone I've met, but I don't remember him."

Dr. G. walked over and took the picture from me. He looked at it for a few moments, and then replaced it on the piano. "This is my grandson, Murray. You might have met him when you were younger, he lived here with me for awhile. He died a few years ago."

"Oh," I said. "I guess I remembered the face from years ago; yeah, I think I remember that scar on his nose."

"He only got that scar a month or so before he died, you probably just remember him from when you were a kid," said Dr. G.

"Speaking of paleontology," said Ryan, "We've come to ask you about any dinosaur digs that might be near by. Austin dreamt about dinosaurs last night so we looked them up on the internet and found out that there was a dig somewhere about."

"Yeah," I added. "I'm probably crazy, but I thought it might have to do with this rock I found."

I took the rock out of my pocket and unwrapped it from the cloth that I had it in. "I found it yesterday and then, last night, I had the weirdest dream about dinosaurs. I've probably been watching too much T. V., but I keep thinking that the rock might have something . . ."

"Get that thing away from me!" Dr. Gerard yelled, backing as far away as possible from the rock and turning very pale. "Bury it deep in a hole and forget you ever saw it! I mean it, kids! That rock is very dangerous and could cause all sorts of trouble! Now get out of here with it! You kids had better get on with your summer and forget all about dinosaurs. It could be dangerous for you to start exploring around. I'm very serious about this," Dr. G. exploded.

"But Dr. G.," Ryan insisted, "You must have worked in that dig with your grandson. It's really exciting and we'd like to know about it."

"Ryan, there are some things that are better left alone," Dr. G. replied. "This is definitely one of them."

What was that all about? He is totally freaked out and I really didn't do anything, it was just a dream. I thought.

"Well, we found a diary entry on the internet, that's what got us interested. It's signed, 'Murray,' and he talks about his granddad, Arthur. Isn't that your name, Dr. G.? Here, take a look at it," Kayla handed him the print out.

I thought he might faint; he got that pale as he read it.

"Where did you find this?" he whispered.

Kayla went over to his computer, "I can find it for you, if you like," she said.

"Yes, please."

She brought it up and we waited until Dr. G. had read the whole thing. When he turned around he seemed kind of stunned.

"Just leave it all alone kids. You don't know what you're digging up here. Please leave it alone." He turned back to the computer.

We stood there for a few minutes, but he seemed to have forgotten we were there, so after a while we left.

"What was that all about?" Kayla asked when we got outside.

"I don't know, but he scared me. What do you think is so frightening about some old bones?" I asked.

"Maybe we should leave it alone. He seemed pretty upset about it."

"You want to leave the mystery unsolved? No way!" Ryan's eyes were sparkling. "What we need to decide is what we do next."

CHAPTER SIX

—◆—

Explorations

"Well, if we're going to keep investigating, let's go back to where you found that rock and snoop around. Maybe there are more of them, they might lead us to the dig." Ryan suggested.

"Yeah, sure," I replied, hardly listening. I was still wondering why Dr. G. was so upset about the rock.

"Let's go tell Grandma that we are off to the beach for the day so she won't worry," said Ryan.

"I want you kids to let me pack a lunch first. It looks like the weather will be nice. You could take the dog with you, she just loves the beach. Make sure you've got towels and go by bike so you can get home quickly if you need to. Wear shorts and a top over your swim suits in case it gets too cool." she said in one big breath, fussing around the kitchen.

Grabbing the bag of things that Grandma gave us, we rode down to where I had found the first rock and started exploring the area off to the side of the road. Just looking around, we all found more sparkling rocks than we had ever realized were there.

"You know," I said, "I'll bet there's nothing at all unusual about the rock I found. There are a lot of them here; they can't all give you strange dreams."

Kayla wasn't listening, "sweeet," she breathed, "These could be real gems, you guys. Look at them sparkle." She gathered samples to take back for Grandpa to see.

Ryan and I glanced over and then continued looking around ourselves.

After awhile, Ryan said, "This is no good. We don't even know what we are looking for. We've climbed a long way up the side of this hill and found nothing. We're all hot and Bessie needs water. I'm going back to where we left the bikes and get her some," he started down the hill.

I kept on searching, if I could just find a rock like the first one.

Ryan came back with water for all of us. He handed me mine and looked around for Kayla.

"Where did she get to?" he asked me.

"I don't know, I haven't seen her for a long time," I said.

"Kayla! Kayla! "Ryan yelled as loud as he could. No answer. He ran farther up the hill side. "Kayla, where are you?"

"Bessie, find Kayla," I said, releasing her from the leash.

Bessie shot up the hill on the run, barking all the way.

The next minute Kayla appeared about one hundred or so yards above us on a trail.

"What's all the noise about? You two have got to come up here and see this cave I've found. I just haven't found the way in yet."

Ryan and I scrambled up to where she stood.

"Every time I looked around, I saw more and better rocks," she said, "then I saw the cave, come on, it's beautiful."

She led us around the corner where she had been and over some boulders to the top of the hill, then she lay down and seemed to peer through the rocks.

"Look, it's absolutely awesome."

I scrunched down beside her and she moved over so that I could put my eye on the opening, I looked in.

"Fantastic," I breathed, "Ryan, you've got to see this." I moved over so he could see too.

Laid out before us was a wonderland of light. A sunbeam hit the cave from another hole and the rocks seemed to light up on there own. There was color everywhere, but the over all effect was a sort of green, like you see in the depths of a spring forest. A stream glistened on the cave floor, running into the darkness. We just lay there, gazing at it all.

"This is magnificent." I breathed, "We've got to get inside somehow,"

We started around the narrow path that Kayla had been on. We tried to move some rocks, out of the way if we saw a likely spot, but they were all too big for us to lift.

"This is just frustrating. We'll have to work out a better plan and try again tomorrow," Kayla said, "I'll get Bessie." She called her, but there was no answer. We walked down to the bikes, but she wasn't there either.

"She's got to be up at the cave, she's just run on ahead," Kayla said. "Let's go back up."

We climbed back again, following that narrow trail and calling all the way. As we neared the top of the hill, still calling, a dog barked.

"Did you hear that," Ryan said, "a dog barking, only far away?"

We all listened.

"Yeah, I hear it too, but that dog is really far away." I said.

We all called together.

The dog bark came back to us right away.

"She must have run on towards home ahead of us. Let's go down again and head there too, she'll meet us on the way I bet," said Kayla.

We headed down, calling every now and then.

"You know what," I said, "that bark is sounding farther away now, maybe she's stuck somewhere on the top of the hill. There's lots of crags and crevasses that she could have fallen into up there."

We turned around and headed back up the hill.

Searching the rocks proved easier that we thought because the dog kept barking to us. Her voice was getting stronger and stronger. Finally, Kayla looked into a small hole in the rocky expanse and saw the tubby little creature staring back at her.

"Bessie, how on earth did you get in there?"

"There has got to be a bigger hole, she's one fat dog. If she got in there, so can we," Ryan said.

"You're right," I agreed, "let's find it."

Now that we knew what we were looking for it was much easier. After about five minutes, Ryan had found the hole that Bessie likely went down.

"It's not very big, you guys, maybe we can dig it out a bit and squeeze in easily enough."

"That's a plan," Kayla replied, "I should fit."

She was into the hole after just a few more minutes and yelling back to us.

"There's a ledge here that I can stand on," she said, "across the way I can see where it leads down a tunnel to the cave. I'm going to keep going."

That's when we heard Bessie bark again and the next thing we knew, there was Bessie, heading straight for Kayla, her tail wagging.

CHAPTER SEVEN

Into the Cave

"Be careful," I hollered, "I'm coming in now too."

I started into the hole that Ryan and I had expanded, and soon found myself standing on the ledge. I turned around to let Ryan know that I was okay but I slipped and lost my balance.

I yelled as I fell, but it turned out to be only about six feet or so to the tunnel floor. I stood up and shook myself off.

"Austin, you okay, man?" Ryan asked as he climbed into the tunnel too.

"I'm okay, I don't think I'm hurt."

"Your arm is bleeding," said Ryan, "and you've ripped your shorts."

I looked at my arm.

"Must have cut it on a sharp rock, but it's not deep. Kayla is ahead of us, let's catch up," I said.

As we walked, we looked around.

"These rocks are huge and really full of mica. It's awesome down here," I said.

"Yeah, no wonder someone built this tunnel," said Ryan. He had turned on his flashlight.

"A flashlight, you think of everything, dude," I said to him. "How far to the cave I wonder?"

I didn't quite hear his answer. I felt dizzy and like I might be sick. The next minute I passed out.

When I came to, Ryan and Kayla were both gone and I didn't know where I was. Then I heard Kayla.

"Come on, Austin, you've got to see this place. It is so rad!" She seemed to be yelling from far away. "Hey, come on! We've reached the cave! It's even better when you're right in it! Hurry up!"

I stumbled forwards, following the dim glow from Ryan's flashlight and listening to them talking.

"Are you coming?" Kayla called.

"I'm just about there," I shouted back.

As soon as I got to the cave, I could see how amazing it was. It was truly beautiful. I guess I had run too fast because my palms began to sweat and I felt my heart racing. The dizziness came back too, but this time it just sort of stayed.

"What's happening, guys?" I whispered.

"Look at the walls. They're gleaming, and the floor is shiny, too. I can hardly tell if it's rock or glimmering water," said Kayla.

I looked again, and gasped as a tingle ran up my spine. The whole of the cave shone, from the ceiling to the floor. The tunnel walls glowed with a greenish, eerie light. Awestruck, all three of us stood and stared for a few minutes. Then I saw the dinosaurs moving on the cave walls. As I stared I could see the dinosaurs, the forest, the swamp and the ocean, just like in my dream. It seemed to me that I could have walked right through those walls and been back in that land again.

"Hey, you guys, I can see the dinosaur land from my dream, right here on the tunnel walls, weird, huh?" I said quietly, no one heard me.

Kayla had run on ahead again and now she called back to us. "Look, over here, there's another tunnel leading upwards. I wonder where it goes."

I was watching as the dinosaurs grazed on the tunnel walls. I felt drawn towards them and wanted to touch them. I reached out my hand towards the wall and gasped. This time, Ryan did hear me.

"What's wrong?" he asked.

"Look," I replied.

We both looked at my hand. It had gone a scaly blue grey with little spiky things growing out of the back of it. My fingers were getting longer and thinner with real claws on the ends. Ryan turned white as a ghost and gasped for breath. I felt sweaty all over, and my mind seemed to be in a fog.

"*Where am I?*" I wondered.

"What's happening?" asked Ryan, looking kind of sick.

"I don't know, what's happening to me?" I could feel the tears just behind my eyes.

"We've got to get you out of here, Austin," said Ryan.

Kayla yelled back to us, "Hey, there's a trap door up here."

"Kayla, come back. We have to get Austin out of here now!" called Ryan.

"Just give me a sec," Kayla said. A moment later we heard a slam and Kayla came around the corner running very fast. She reached us and ran straight past us, up the tunnel, going at full speed. Finally she stopped, turned around and came back to us.

"Do you know who was in that room?" she blurted out, panting hard.

"Let's just get Austin out of here; we'll talk later."

She glanced at me, then stopped and stared. "What's happened?"

"We don't know. Help me to get him out of here," said Ryan.

"But what's wrong with your hands, Austin? You look like some kind of monster."

"Shut up and help me," snapped Ryan, "You take his left side and I'll stay on the right.

She did what she was told. We limped up the tunnel that way.

When we reached the hole, we realized that it was too far up to climb out.

I fell to the ground. I seemed to shift back and forth from the cave to the land of the dinosaurs. Sometimes I was munching grass with the herd, and then, in a flash of light, I would be lying on the floor of the cave, listening to the conversation.

"How do we—out? Look at him.—if we get him out,—do with him?"

The scene faded and I was with my scared friend from the jungle again. A few moments later and a flash of light brought me back to the cave.

"What's—now?" said Kayla. "He's not holding—rocks."

"That's it!" Ryan yelled. "It's the cuts;—by the rocks—he fell.—have to clean—."

I heard feet running and then silence.

Now my dinosaur friend was rolling in some herbal plant, showing me a sore on his side now covered in the herb. As I looked at him, I knew that I knew someone just like him, somewhere else.

A flash of light.

". . . only Bessie's water, but it's . . . have to do," Kayla's voice said from a distance.

Something was rubbing on my arms and legs, but I couldn't make out what it was.

CHAPTER EIGHT

Back to Reality

Another flash of light; then Ryan's voice, "Did you see that, his skin was green, it's turning back to normal now. I think the washing is helping a lot."

"Yeah," said Kayla, "and that downy fuzz on his body seems to be going away as well."

Ryan spoke again, "The freakiest thing was that big lump on his nose, thank goodness it washed away too," he said.

"Oh, look," said Kayla, "you're awake, Austin, welcome back to reality; you were pretty out of it for awhile."

Ryan took off his shorts, standing only in his swim trunks, he handed the shorts to me. "You'd better put these on," he said.

"What . . . ? Oh," I said, looking down to where my own clothes hung in rags from my waist, "Thanks."

"We need to get out of this hole," said Kayla.

"Kayla, I'll boost you up first, go find a rope or something we can use to get out of here," said Ryan.

Kayla climbed out on Ryan's shoulders. She reached the top with no problem.

I could hear Bessie bounding around with excitement as she saw Kayla come over the edge. We waited in silence for awhile, then we could hear running above our heads. Kayla was back, with Bessie's leash in her hand.

"I've tied the far end to a pretty sturdy tree," she said, "it's holding solid, I think. Ryan, let's see if we can get Austin up together."

Ryan hoisted me up around the waist, I grabbed the leash and Kayla pulled. I tried to scramble up as much as I could, but Kayla did a lot of the work. Finally I was out. Getting Ryan out was a lot easier. He was able to hang on to the leash and climb out using the side of the wall to support his legs.

We sat down on the grass at the top to catch our breath. Kayla looked me over for cuts.

"Wow, what happened to you, Austin?" asked Ryan? "I have never been so scared in my whole life!"

"I wish I knew," I said, "Maybe Dr. G. is right and this is too dangerous to pursue."

"It's impossible that you can really change into a dinosaur, Austin," said Kayla "isn't it?"

"I don't know, it sure seems that I was one, it's so scary and weird. I just don't get it at all. It's frightening me, what if I hadn't changed back to myself?"

"Well, it sure scared me to see you changing like that," she muttered.

There wasn't really much else to say. We walked down to the beach and sat on the sand, looking out over the lake at the sparkling water. It was a fantastic place to be. We sat there in the sun for awhile and Kayla told us her part of the story. When she went to the end of that tunnel she was exploring, she found a trap door in the ceiling of the tunnel. Of course she just had to open it. When she did, she recognized the room above as the living room of the manor house. She knew it by the unusual fire place. She also saw someone sitting beside the fireplace and staring straight at her. She didn't recognize who it was because it all happened so fast. Kayla slammed the door down again, fast. That was the noise we had heard. A few minutes later she had caught up with Ryan and me.

"Oh boy," said Ryan, "Trouble, I think."

"Yeah, I was thinking the same thing," I added.

We were all quiet for a bit, after awhile my thoughts went to the dinosaur with the scar on his face. He really reminded me of that picture of Dr. G.'s grandson, Murray. I wasn't sure though, it could have been just my imagination.

Should I say something to Ryan and Kayla? No, it's too wild to talk about right now. If I ever get to go back to the dinosaurs again, and if I see him there, I'll tell them, but not now.

Ryan broke the silence, "This is getting so weird; do we need to talk to Dr. G. again?"

"What will we tell him?" asked Kayla, "Instead of leaving the whole mess alone like you told us to, we went and discovered a tunnel and cave.

Oh, yeah, and by the way, Austin kept seeing dinosaurs on the walls of the cave, then he nearly turned into a dinosaur himself." Kayla just shook her head. "We can't very well do that now, can we?"

"You're right Kayla," I said. "Let's leave him out of it if we can." I replied.

"I think we should just forget it and get on with our summer. Let's go for a swim," said Kayla.

As she got up, we all heard a rustle in the bushes behind us. We turned to see Eric standing there. He didn't say anything; he just smiled at us, and walked over to the parking lot.

I felt my heart start to race at the sight of him. I glanced at Kayla, she had gone quite pale.

"Now I know who saw me when I poked my head into their living room, it was Eric." she said. Ryan looked at both of us. "Big trouble," he muttered.

CHAPTER NINE

Big Trouble

The next morning the phone rang before eight. Grandma answered it and said it was for me. It was Dr. G. He asked me to come over; he said that he needed to talk to me NOW!

"What did Dr. Gerard want, Austin?" asked Grandma.

I felt ill. My mouth went dry. I turned to the toaster and put in a couple of slices of bread, that way I didn't have to look at Grandma while we talked.

"Oh, it's nothing. Just some rocks that he wants to show me," I said, and then I added to the lie. "I told him I would come over yesterday, but I didn't get there. I guess he's a bit ticked at me."

"Don't you go annoying that man, Austin," she replied, setting the table, "He's kind and gentle and this town doesn't always treat him well."

"I know, Grandma, I'll be nice to him," I promised.

"Austin, I got a call from your mom last night while you kids were out. She's on her way, and she's bringing Kevin," Grandma told me, "they'll be arriving around three. Make sure that you're back here."

"Yeah, okay," I replied, we both sat down at the table to eat. "Do you think they're going to get married soon?"

"Do you have some worries about it, Austin?" she asked.

"No, not really, it will just be different, I guess," I said.

But the truth was that even though Kevin is polite enough, I can't stand him and I think he feels the same about me. I think he loves Mom and all, and I know he's trying to be nice to me, I think he just does it to make Mom like him more. Sometimes he forget and acts like my Dad, bossing me around and then telling me that he likes me. I hate that.

We'll be moving to his house, in a new area for me. I didn't want to go to a new school. I've got friends where I am now. I know I can visit them, but it will be very different. Mom says I'm just being selfish, but I can't help it.

"Well, you better get a move on and see what Dr. Gerard has to say to you," Grandma said.

"Kayla, Ryan, get up, we have to go," I shouted. I didn't want to have to see Dr. G. alone.

They were up like a shot and grabbing toast. Ryan put one of Grandma's fat sausages on it and Kayla grabbed a hard boiled egg. I settled for peanut butter for my last piece, the sausages seemed greasier than usual.

Bessie followed us out the door, hoping for handouts. As we got onto our bikes, I told them about the phone call.

"I knew Eric saw me yesterday," Kayla said.

"I wonder how much he heard at the beach, he must have been listening." Ryan said. "It was too much of a coincidence that he appeared so suddenly,"

"Yeah, I think so too," I replied, "I'm sure glad that you guys are with me."

Dr. G. met us at the top gate. He was alone, pacing the walkway. He walked quickly toward me.

"Austin," he said sternly, "Eric says he saw Kayla at my trap door and then heard you talking together at the beach. I want you to tell me what Eric heard you saying yesterday, also, who else knows besides these two?" He glared at Kayla and Ryan.

My hands felt sweaty and my heart beat fast. I started to stammer, "I h-h-haven't told—."

"Careful what you say, Austin; just let me know how you found the dinosaur dig and what happened there," Dr. G. demanded. I knew that he would see through a lie.

"We learned about the dig on the web," I muttered without looking at him.

"You can do better than that, Austin. Eric tells me that you were there; he saw Kayla from the trap door. That's trespassing, for starters!" He looked angry now, his face red and frowning.

"Eric doesn't know everything," I yelled, "we didn't go there without a reason."

"What kind of reason could you possibly have had?" he snapped back.

"Well, you know that I had that dream about being a dinosaur. It seemed more real than dreamlike though. Then we looked it up on the internet and found out what the kind of dinosaur I was, in the dream. When I saw a picture of it, I knew I was a Hadrosaurus. Then we found that diary about dinosaurs at Shadow Lake," I rushed on, "we just wanted to know if that dig really existed, so we decided to try to look for it."

Dr. G. grabbed me by the shoulders and made me look right into his angry eyes. "Eric said that you talked about visiting the land of the dinosaurs. What about that?"

"It was a dream. In the dream I visited the dinosaurs. I just told you. It felt like I was one of them. I know it was just a dream, but it felt real." I could feel the tears welling up as I lied to him. I could tell him about finding the cave, but I couldn't tell him what had happened in there.

I thought Dr. G. was going to yell, but he just stared at me for several moments; then, very quietly, he said. "Austin, I need the truth from you about this. You had better all come inside and tell me everything."

We walked silently down the driveway and into the house.

He's going to find out anyway, I may as well tell him everything.

Eric was sitting in the kitchen when we got there.

Not him. I really don't want to let him in on all of this.

"Dr. G., can't I just tell the story to you, not everyone else?" I asked, glaring at Eric.

"Eric stays, we need to get it all straight," he said.

"But, it's really not his business, he's not a part of it," I replied.

"It is and he stays," said Dr.G.

I glared at Eric as I started to talk. He looked back at me with a smirk on his face.

"We found a cave yesterday . . ." I poured out the story, trying not to think about Eric being there. It took about half an hour to tell the whole thing. Each time I glanced at Dr. G., he looked paler and sicker. I paced the length of the kitchen, looking out the window at the hillside brush turning yellow as it began to flower, watching the kettle steam quietly on the stove.

Dr. G. looked really sick by the time I got to the end. He slid into a chair and put his head in his hands. Kayla went over and sat down beside him. Eric pushed her aside, sitting down in her chair and taking Dr. G.'s hand. I didn't know what else to do so I just stopped talking.

"—and then we came over here when you called this morning," I said.

"Who else knows about this?" Dr. G. groaned.

"Well, Eric overheard us, and now, you." I said.

There was silence. Finally Dr. G. said, "Austin, did you bring the rock that you showed me two days ago? May I please see it again?"

"It's right here, Dr. G.," I replied, pulling it out of my pocket, still wrapped in the cloth I had put it into, I handed it to him. He opened it carefully and turned it over and over in his hand.

"Be careful," I yelled. I reached to grab the rock back, but he held it out of my grasp.

He didn't have any right to take it away from me. That was my rock.

I stepped closer to him and grabbed for it again.

"You could turn into a dinosaur you know," I shouted as he pulled away from me again.

"Is that what really happened to you, Austin?" he asked.

"Yes, I think so." I whispered.

"It can't affect me, it only ever affected Murray," he said quietly.

"Who?" I asked.

"My grandson, Murray," he said.

"Oh, yeah," I said, remembering, "Dr. G., this will sound ridiculous, but one of the dinosaurs I saw reminds me of the picture of your grandson Murray."

Dr. G. stared at me for a long time, and then he sighed. He seemed to finally accept what he was hearing. He held out the rock to me.

CHAPTER TEN

A Demonstration

"Would you be willing to show me what happens when you hold it Austin?" he asked, quietly.

"When I first held it I felt dizzy right away," I said, I grabbed the rock from him, glad to have it back. "Yesterday was stranger. I put the rock under my pillow, before I went to bed. Maybe I can make the rock do it again. You guys take the rock away from me if I get too bizarre." I could hardly get the last words out, I was feeling so dizzy.

"Okay, we've got your back," Kayla replied. Ryan nodded his head.

Suddenly I was back in the swamp. The water glistened in the sun, off to my right. I started towards it. The sky seemed to go on forever, getting bluer and bluer. The sun shone brightly and left rays of itself mirrored in the water. I could feel the breeze on my face and body, and it smelled wonderful.

This place feels like the world should feel. It's so nice and fresh. I don't know which I like better, here or back home.

My body felt heavy and strange. I looked at my legs and feet. They were huge and green and scaly! UGH! I lumbered over to the water and looked in. My reflection stared back at me. For a split second, I knew that I was a dinosaur! What a face, with a long jaw bone, flat teeth, a neck that went on forever and a horn on my head.

As quickly as I recognized this reflection of myself, the idea was gone. All I could understand was that I was in a happy and comfortable space. The water invited me in. It looked so cool. I wanted to feel it on my skin. I wanted the sensation of floating, almost weightless, in the soft waves. I waded and soaked in the salty water, floating, swimming and playing with the limbs of trees that had fallen in.

Suddenly, from behind, I heard a terrible roar. I panicked and swam for shore. Whatever was following me had huge jaws. I could hear them snapping just behind me. I glanced back and caught a glimpse of a massive sea creature snapping at my back. My blood felt icy cold. I swam for my life. Finally I reached the shore and climbed out; then I looked back, toward the water.

A dinosaur that looked just like me was in the water, fighting the sea creature. He was a young dinosaur and he was putting up a good fight. Those giant jaws snapped at him over and over again. He was bleeding from his back and legs. Finally, the dinosaur grabbed the sea creature by the neck and would not let go. As I watched, I saw the dinosaur shake the creature's neck until it snapped and I knew the fight was over.

Then I realized that there was a group of young dinosaurs on the shore behind me; some of them headed into the water. I tried to go in with them to see if I could help, but the others blocked my way with their bodies, growling and snarling. I could only watch as others helped. Once on shore, they rubbed leaves and reeds onto his skin. He didn't even try to get up. I had a cold sick feeling inside. I tried once more to go to him, but was forced away again. One of the other males banged against me with a loud rumble coming from his horn. I broke away and ran as fast as possible into the swamp and forest. Then, in a flash of light, I was back in the kitchen.

"You were panting hard and your legs were kicking, so I took the rock away and you seemed to quiet and return to yourself," Kayla said. "We washed your face and hands and your dinosaur parts disappeared, just like they did when you were in the cave."

"You had a lump on the top of your head and were starting to turn greenish," said Dr. G., looking sick and scared.

"Now do you see how weird this all is?" I asked him.

"You must never tell anyone else about this," said Dr. G. "Give me the rock. I'll bury it. Get on with your real life, Austin. This will lead to nothing but trouble!"

I did not hand it over to him.

"Even if I were to destroy this rock, Dr. G., there are many more of them in and around that cave and they can transport me back to the dinosaurs too." I said. "I'm afraid of it, but I am so curious to find out more. Just think of how much I could discover about the dinosaur world if I continue to spend time with them."

"You remind me of Murray, when you say that, Austin," said Dr. G.

For a few minutes he and I looked at each other. No one spoke.

CHAPTER ELEVEN

About Murray

After a moment, I asked, "What happened to your grandson Dr. G.?"

Dr. G. got up and walked over to the piano and picked up the picture of Murray. He looked at it as he started to talk.

"He was able to go to the world of the dinosaurs too, Austin, and he loved it. The first time he went to the land of the dinosaurs, it was with a rock just like yours. The rocks have a special look to them, a kind of glow, that's how I knew what your rock was as soon as you showed it to me. Once he had been to the land of the dinosaurs he did exactly what you kids did; he looked for more rocks; something to explain the connection. One day he found the cave. We started to explore it a bit."

Murray was obsessed with the cave. I didn't really know why, because he hadn't told me that he could see the dinosaurs on the walls. By the time he did tell me, he could feel himself go into the dinosaur world from the cave. After that he knew that he could get to the dinosaurs just by going into the cave. He was delighted. I was scared. From then on I always went with him and when I saw him changing and thought he was getting into trouble, I would bring him back to the house. That was when he made that trap door and ladder that you came up, Kayla, so that he could get in and out more easily. He went there a lot. We didn't have a good system of bringing him back. Getting him away from there helped, but sometimes it took hours for him to return to normal. He told me about the trips to the dinosaur world. He really loved it. I'm afraid I was worried and fretted a lot."

That's why he started going to the cave without telling me. I would be busy with something else and find him gone when I went looking for him. I would go to the cave immediately. I always found him right away. Usually he was lying peacefully on the cave floor. He seemed to be sleeping. I would drag him out and clean him up a bit and he would come back to himself."

"One day I was out in the garden for a few hours. When I came back, he was gone. I rushed to the cave with a bad feeling in my gut. When I came upon him, it terrified me. What I saw was a big dinosaur lying on its side on the cave floor. I called to him to try to wake him, but he didn't stir. Gradually I began to realize that he was dead or nearly dead. I walked towards him and poked at his belly with a stick. Nothing happened. I got a bit more courageous and poked harder. Still nothing happened. I went up to his head, I couldn't detect any breathing. I looked into his eyes. I knew that it was him, even though everything else about him was dinosaur. He was a grayish, green color with thick, scaly skin; there was a horn on his head and his feet were thick and huge. His arms were small and shriveled up, his fingers and toes were claws."

"I was stuck to the spot, unable to move as the horror of it sunk into my mind. I stood there for a long time, looking at him. After a while I sat down on the ground and mumbled over and over, "Let him come back, let him come back.""

"I noticed a deep claw slash right across his face. It ran from below his right eye across his nose and down to his chin. I was frozen with shock and by an overwhelming sense of helplessness. There was nothing I could do. The next time I got up and went over to him he was already dead. I cried and called to him for a long time. Finally I calmed down enough to realize that I had to handle the situation."

"I went to the house and got some hot soapy water to wash the blood from his face. I began to notice, right away that the parts I washed started to lose their dinosaur features and return to the Murray that I knew. I washed his whole body, then I was able to realize that he was not going to change anymore. He was close to the Murray that I loved again; but, as far as I knew, he was still dead. I saw him twitch once and there was a flash of light at the same time. I hid and waited, but nothing happened."

"Through my sorrow, I wondered what to do with the body. I didn't sleep all night, just sat beside him, holding onto his misshapen hand and thinking. By morning I had a plan in mind, but I was still numb with sorrow."

"I spent the next few days digging his grave deep in the dinosaur cave; I buried him by myself, with a prayer and a hymn, then I went upstairs and called the police. I reported him as a missing person."

"Since then the people around here have been gossiping. They say I forced him to leave, somehow that's what hurts worst of all. Now very few people visit me, and many won't let their kids or grandkids visit. I have so much to share with the children, all of my gems and rocks, the history of this town. If they could visit me, it would be so much better. It's only the rare person who still allows it; like your grandparents. Anyway, that's why I am so concerned about you, Austin, and your use of that stone and the cave."

"Could I see the picture again?" I asked.

He handed it to me and I looked into those familiar eyes.

CHAPTER TWELVE

Plans for a meeting

"That's awful, Dr. G." said Kayla, tears glistening in her eyes. "I can't imagine how you managed. It's so sad and you were all alone."

"Granddad gets by all right, he's smart and strong and he's always got me, even if I'm in the city in the winter." He smiled at his grandfather."

"Wow, no wonder the rock I found freaked you out. I wish I knew a way we could help you get back in with the town's people," I said. "Now that I can visit the dinosaurs too, maybe people will be more willing to understand what happened. I could talk to them, I could show them."

"NO! That secret stays with us! It must not go any further," Dr. G. shouted. No one spoke for a minute and then Ryan quietly said, "The world might make some important discoveries from being able to go back to the dinosaurs. Austin, you tell us a lot. You've changed too; you hardly eat any meat now."

"I think that's because I'm a plant eating dinosaur," I muttered, "and after what I've seen of meat eaters, I don't think I want to eat meat."

"All right then, Ryan, what would you do with the discovery? What changes would you make? Start with our little town, right here," said Kayla.

"I think that I'd come and talk to you, Dr. G.; you're the expert on dinosaur digs and rocks. You know what they can teach us."

"I don't think it's worth pursuing, Ryan," said Dr. G., "If it was an ordinary dinosaur graveyard, yes, we would want to inform the paleontologists, but this one is that glowing cave. If people knew that they might be able to travel to the time of the dinosaurs, what would happen? If both Murray and Austin can do it, then some of them would be able to do it too. I think we should leave it alone, and since I own it, that's my decision. Remember all of you are sworn to secrecy," said Dr. G.

"You're right," said Kayla, "you are in charge; we'll just forget it now."

As we got up to leave, dragging our disappointment with us, Eric spoke.

"Granddad, if Austin could tell a few of the town's people what he can do, maybe they would begin to accept the true story of what happened to Murray. It's worth a try."

I turned back, excited. "We wouldn't be telling them, I could really show them and then they would have to believe."

"Or they could say that we were both crazy and you would be an outcast too, Austin, you don't want that, do you?" Dr. G. seemed quite angry.

"What if you were to select who we should tell? Could you choose a few people to hear the story?" Eric asked.

"I just told you that I don't trust anyone around here," Dr. G. shot back.

"That's not quite true though," Ryan said. "What about your friend, Graham? He's over here most days. What about our grandparents, they visit you all year round and they let us come over here on our own."

Dr. G. thought for a moment, "Your grand parents and some other folks need to know what's going on, so we should talk to them. Graham is really trustworthy and he's a loner too, he'd be okay, I think. That's it though, no one else."

"Okay by me. What are we going to say, how will we convince them?" I asked.

CHAPTER THIRTEEN

Changes

"My, you were an awfully long time at Dr. G.'s place, kids," said Grandma as we ran onto the patio. Mom had arrived and of course Kevin was with her.

"We got talking about rocks and stuff, you know how he is, and it's so interesting," I said.

"Hi Austin," Mom said from the other side of the room.

"Hi Mom," I said going over to hug her. "I really miss you. How long can you stay?"

"One thing at a time, Austin. It's wonderful to see you too, son. I miss you when you're away. We'll be here all week, but we have to go back to work next Monday."

I started to choke up. I put my arm around her waist and sat up beside her on the lounge chair. I wondered if I could tell her everything that had been going on.

No, I can't, not yet.

Kevin came over to me and stuck out his hand. "Hi Austin," he said, "It's good to see you.

Yeah, I'll bet you really missed me, eh, with all that alone time with Mom? I gave him a hand shake and said, "Hi, Kevin, I'm glad that you could come too."

"We're both glad to be here, Austin," he replied.

"How about some iced tea," Grandma said, putting a tray of glasses on the table.

When everyone was served, and the chatter about travel and roads had died down, Mom said, "Kevin and I have something to tell you that I hope you will be pleased to hear." She looked over and smiled at him.

She should have talked what ever it is, over with me, before letting the whole family in on it. I just know they're getting engaged. I don't know how to deal with it yet. It's too soon."

"Austin," Kevin said, looking straight at me, "I've asked your Mom to marry me and she has said yes, but only with your approval. Can I please have your Mother as my wife and you as my son?"

I stared at him. I had known they were getting serious, but I really hadn't expected this, in front of everyone. I wanted to talk it over with Mom alone, and then with Kevin. It would mean so many changes for me. Kevin lives right across town from us. I would have to adjust to a new neighborhood, a new school, living farther away from my crowd, and even having Kevin around all the time. I like his house better than ours, it's bigger, but there are all those other things. When they are together, it feels like he's sooo important and I'm just invisible.

I didn't want to spoil their moment; I smiled at both of them and said, "Sure I approve. When will you get married?"

"We haven't decided that yet. I think that all of us will need time to get used to the changes," said Mom, "It's likely more than a year away."

Well that's a relief anyway.

"We want to do things one step at a time," said Kevin, getting down on one knee in front of Mom. "Ann, will you marry me?"

Mom looked at him and I could see in her eyes that she really wanted this. "Yes, I will," she said quietly.

Kevin pulled a fabulous ring out of his pocket and slipped it onto her finger. It was too small, so he put it onto her baby finger instead of her ring finger. There were hugs and kisses all around. Grandma started crying and then she and Mom started talking about weddings and dresses and stuff.

Hey! What happened to waiting a whole year?

After a few minutes, Ryan, Kayla and I slipped away and went to the far corner of the yard.

"Wow," said Kayla, "Things are really changing for you, eh, Austin?"

"Yeah," I replied, not to enthusiastically. I started pulling blades of grass from the lawn.

"It'll be okay," she smiled at me, I thought I might cry at any second. We sat quietly together for a while.

"Can I ask you about something completely different?" asked Ryan. "Did you visit the dinosaurs last night?"

"Yeah, I did. I guess I should have told you guys, but it was sort of spontaneous."

"Austin, please come and get one of us if you feel like a trip to dinosaur land. It's so much safer if we are there to pull the rock away from you," said Ryan.

"Yeah, fine, I don't think it's that big a deal, but if it will make you feel better, I'll let you know." I said.

"It will," they both replied together.

"Anyway, it was a good trip," I said, "That dinosaur that got hurt is looking stronger now. He's still limping, though, and having trouble keeping up with the group on the run. The adult males are protecting him. He's doing okay. I sure hope he recovers soon."

"Why?" asked Kayla.

"The dinosaurs my age hang around together and I'm being shoved out of the group," I replied, "I guess they blame me for what happened to their friend. I think they know I'm not really one of them. I arrive fully developed and I'm only there part of the time; they've noticed. Maybe when the injured one gets better I'll be included. I sure hope so."

CHAPTER FOURTEEN

Depression

The next day, Mom said, "Kevin and I are going up to visit the Russell's." Would you like to come, Austin?"

I don't' want to visit with adults that I don't know very well? It felt like she was planning something that she knew I wouldn't be interested in. She just wanted to be with Kevin.

"No thanks, I'm going to the beach with Kayla and Ryan," I replied.

Kevin's being there was already changing things. I don't want to do stuff with him and Mom. I wanted to spend time with MY MOM, just the two of us. Couldn't she see that? Didn't she remember how much fun we used to have?

"What are you so sulky about?" asked Ryan, as he came into the kitchen.

"Does it show that badly?" I asked. "I'm ticked off at Mom and Kevin. They're always together; you'd think she'd have a minute or two for me, without him around."

"Well, I think you need to get used to it, it could get worse," said Ryan.

"Thanks, I needed that."

"Sorry. Let's throw the football around while Kayla finishes dressing," he replied.

We went to the front yard. It was nearly the size of a football field. We warmed up with some tosses. Ryan threw one into the far corner of the yard and then noticed the crumpled spot in the grass.

"What happened here?" he asked. "It looks like something was lying out here all night. Do you think a deer or a bear was around?"

"Not likely, someone just left something on the ground overnight and picked it up this morning," I said, not wanting to admit that I had spent the night outside.

"I don't think so," Ryan replied, "It's really broken down; we should tell Grandpa about it."

I couldn't let him do that so I decided on the truth.

"Ryan, if I tell you a secret will you promise to keep it?" I asked.

"Sure, so long as it's not dangerous or anything," he replied.

"Okay, I've been sleeping out here for the past few days."

"You've what?"

"Cool it, will you" I said, "I've been sleeping out here. It feels good under the stars and near the trees."

"Why didn't you say something?"

"Hey, I'll bet Grandma and Grandpa would have let us set up a tent here. That would be fun."

"I don't want you to think I'm stupid or something but I don't want a tent; that would hide the stars and trees."

"Is this something else you've picked up from those darn dinosaurs, Austin? I'm your friend, but they're making you weird, you know that?"

"I know, but I'm not hurting anyone, and I've got to work out this whole double life thing. Just trust me for a while, okay."

"Yeah, okay," muttered Ryan, "but I hope you work it out before the summer is gone."

That afternoon the three of us went down to the beach. The water cooled us off right away. After a hard swim, Ryan and I met some of the other boys and got a game of Frisbee going with lots of splashing and jumps and grabbing at each other. There were quite a lot of weeds in the water and we kept catching ourselves up in them. The other guys got on with the game, but I couldn't ignore those weeds. I started ripping handfuls of them out and diving down to make sure I got the whole thing.

"Hey Austin, what are you doing?" called my friend Kyle. "Are you trying to clean up the whole lake single handedly?"

"Maybe I am. Why don't you guys help too?"

For a few minutes the whole group helped, but they got bored and went back to the game. I kept on pulling weeds. Some of the older women helped me. When Mom and Kevin arrived to get us for dinner, they were impressed and even joined in for awhile. By the time we left, there was quite a pile of weeds."

"Maybe you could get a job as beach cleaner, Austin, and an activity director for old ladies," yelled one of the boys, as we walked away.

CHAPTER FIFTEEN

Boating

The next day turned out even worse. I couldn't stand watching the picnickers' behavior. They sat on their beach mats, eating and drinking, all day and dropping their pop cans and sunscreen bottles on the sand, then they just walked away. I went up and talked to them about it.

"Do you know the damage you are doing to our beautiful beach?" I asked. "This place used to be nicer than you can imagine, with crystal blue water and white sandy beaches. It's people being careless like that, that's made it so polluted. Please don't empty your half full pop cans out on the sand, it attracts flies and bees and dirties the beach. Your sun screen leaks into the sand and damages it. If we don't care for the beach, we will lose it."

Some people were nice about it; others laughed and told me to get a life. I didn't care. I spent most of the day cleaning out the weeds while the other kids played. Why didn't they understand how important this was?

The next morning, Grandpa asked, "While everyone is here, why don't we take the boat for a spin today?"

"That's a good idea, my dear," Grandma said, "Is everyone for it?"

There was unanimous consent and the room started to buzz with boating plans.

"Austin, are you all right with this?" Mom asked me while the others were getting ready, "you don't seem very enthusiastic."

"Yeah, its okay," I replied, "I'm just thinking about how much pollution the boats cause to the lake."

"You never used to worry about that before this summer, what's changed?"

I wanted to tell her. I wanted to show her dinosaur land. I wanted to take her to those wonderful beaches along the ocean front that were covered in shells, not broken bits of shells, but real, whole shells. I wanted her to see the ocean, how blue it was and how many animals, big and small were in it. I wanted her to see that sky and smell the freshness of the air and hear the quietness, but I knew I couldn't.

"I guess I'm just more aware of the pollution problem this summer. Mom, we really could do ourselves in, but nobody seems to notice. It's important, Mom."

She put her arm around me, "I know it is, son, but I wish you could relax and have a bit of fun," she said. Then she went off to find Kevin, right in the middle of our talk! She was obsessed with him. I didn't need another man to share my Mom with, that's for sure.

We drove to the beach. I had to, I didn't know how to get out of it. All day on that boat I just sat and watched the fumes bellow out behind us. I also watched the fumes bellowing from the other boats. I would have much preferred to be rowing or paddling.

What a mess we are making, I thought.

After lunch on a little island in the middle of the lake, Grandpa came and sat down beside me at the back of the boat.

"Hey Austin, what's on your mind, you're awfully quiet?"

"Hi Grandpa," I said, "I'm just thinking about how much we're polluting the lake. Wouldn't it be nice if it was crystal clear and deep blue, like it was meant to be?"

"Well, it's a nice idea, but I don't really think it's practical any more. So many people rely on things that pollute. I wonder if it's even possible to change their minds and their way of life."

"I think it is possible; if we all try hard enough." I replied, "If we all just go along with what everyone else is doing because we think it will never change, it never will. I was dreaming about dinosaurs the other night, and in their world the water was clean and clear."

I couldn't believe what had just escaped from my mouth!

You've got to be more careful, you dope. I thought.

"You're right, we should at least try," Grandpa said. A few minutes later I noticed that he had turned the boat around. We were back at the dock by three p.m.

I want the family to have fun together and relax, but I want our earth to be safe and clean too, I thought.

That night, lying in bed, I realized that I would have to choose. I could either play around with my family and grandparents, or I could try to bring my experience with the dinosaurs and my realization of what pollution was doing to our world, back home. It seemed like, when I tried doing anything to control the pollution, no one wanted to co operate. I tossed and turned trying to think of what to do; it seemed to be an impossible choice. I needed to put it all out of my mind for now. I got up and put the rock under my pillow.

I know that I promised to tell Ryan or Kayla if I wanted to do this again, but tonight I just want to lie here and go to dinosaur land, it will be okay this once, I thought.

I knew that I would be with the dinosaurs soon.

Chapter Sixteen

The Decision

When I arrived back in the dinosaur world, all was quiet and the night was beautiful. The stars were floating just over my head. The moon and the clouds were awesome. I found the herd and slept contentedly.

In the morning, it was time for one of the older dinosaurs's teaching lessons. When I saw him I recognized him. He looked like Murray in that picture. He had that same scar across the nose. I was so startled that I let out a high squeak from my horn. Everyone noticed and stared, so I settled down, and tried to concentrate on what we were doing.

He took us into the swamp. There were flowers blooming there that I had never seen before. He got down on his front legs and took a mouthful, chewed for a moment and then spat them out. Then he encouraged us to taste them and spit them out. It was easy to spit them out, they tasted awful! Another lesson, don't eat these flowers, they won't kill you but they taste bad.

We stayed in the swamp, rolling around in the mud, all afternoon I was not welcomed by the group, but I wasn't attacked either. The dinosaur that had saved my life was there and looking better. He came over to me and I looked at him. He stood still and let me walk around him so that I could see how well he was healing. He looked pretty good. I nuzzled him under his chin and he nuzzled me back. After that, the rest of the group seemed okay with me. Then I was back in my own bed and it was morning. The rock had once again fallen to the floor.

"Well, you must have decided to sleep indoors with the rest of us," said Ryan. We were both at the bathroom sink, brushing our teeth.

"I went to visit the dinosaurs last night," I told him.

"Without telling me or Kayla?" he hissed.

"I made a last minute decision and you guys were both asleep already," I replied.

"Austin, you can't just do that, okay? What if you had gotten into trouble?" Ryan asked.

"But I didn't," I snapped back, "I'm good."

"You're supposed to let Kayla and I know when you are going there. We can't help you if we don't know where you are. It gets dangerous there pretty fast, from what I've seen." Ryan said.

"Sorry" I muttered.

"That's twice you've not let us know what's happening. Promise me that you'll always tell us from now on," Ryan was upset.

"Yeah, Okay," I told him.

One more dreary day went by, with me and a few of the ladies cleaning weeds, while the group had fun. Nothing seemed to be happening about our meeting with Dr. G. and Eric. We hadn't even heard from them. By dinner time I was really down.

Maybe I could go live with the dinosaurs full time, I thought, *then I wouldn't have any more worries about pollution, or Kevin or anything; just that peaceful, fun existence with my group. There would be sad times and dangerous times, but I wouldn't have long term problems to solve and hard relationships to work out.* The more I thought about it, the better I liked the idea.

That night, I snuck out onto the lawn again and planned what to do. After awhile I went back into the house and got a paper and pen from the kitchen. Using a miniature flashlight, I wrote a long letter to Mom, explaining everything, and telling her that I was going back to the dinosaurs for good. That way she and Kevin could be together with no worries about me.

I left the letter on the patio table, with a stone on top of it. I was crying when I left, but this seemed the only way. I walked over to the tunnels and climbed into the cave. I had the rock in my pocket, in case I needed it. I walked farther into the cave than I had gone before, looking for a small private nook in which to make the change. It was really dark and scary down there, but I thought it would be a good hiding place. I didn't want them finding me and bringing me back . . . at least not right away. The change started very soon after I entered the cave, but I persisted in finding a safe and remote corner. Finally, I found where I wanted to be. For luck, I touched the rock and felt myself changing. I was entering the world of the dinosaurs and this time there was no going back.

CHAPTER SEVENTEEN

Living in the Past

It was night when I arrived. The herd was all around me. I stood there and looked at the stars and tree tops that I had come to love, and I fell asleep. At first light, the herd was awake and moving. I was hungry; munching along while slowly rambling through the trees and onto the plains was nice. I ate my fill, savoring every bite, and then I joined my group at the lake. After a long drink and an invigorating swim, we settled in the mud for a cooling bath. The dinosaur that saved me was beside me again, nudging me into a game of splash. Others joined in, too.

Soon the teacher came by and we went into the forest with him. This time he took us to a secluded and forested beach where we could see some large circular mounds in the sand. As we got closer these began to look more like sand nests and sure enough, there were eggs in them. There were maybe six eggs in each nest. I realized right away that these were the eggs of our herd. I don't know how I knew it, maybe it was their brown and green speckled color, or their shape, but something in my heart knew right away that they were ours. The Teacher nudged one with his nose and rolled it over.

One of our group went to do the same, but The Teacher bellowed and nudged him away. He looked at us, took a step towards the eggs and looked back at us. A few of us moved cautiously toward the eggs. Soon we were all around the nests. It felt like a solemn time. These were to be our descendants; they would become part of the herd.

The rest of the day was spent eating and playing in the water and mud. As night fell, we gathered into the herd again and slept. It felt very peaceful, yet something was troubling me, I could feel it, but I couldn't tell what it was.

Morning brought a feeling of tension that ran through everyone. We stayed close together and ate little. I tried to go down by the sand but I was butted back into the forest by an adult male. I noticed that this happened to others of my group as well.

In the air, I could smell something new. Where had I smelled that smell before? Then I recognized it! The day the meat eater had chased us and caught, and eaten, that older female. That's where I knew it from. My heart felt tight and my mouth was dry. In the distance, I could hear the thundering of a strange dinosaur. Our herd leader blared and we were running for our lives.

The enemy was larger than the last one had been, and faster. I kept an eye on the dinosaur that had saved me. He was slow, but managed to stay within the inner circle. The older males kept prodding him on with their horn, forcing him to keep going. It was over as suddenly as it had started. With a mighty yell, another female fell. I looked back to see a gruesome, blood spattered sight as the monster bit into her flesh again and again, ripping off huge pieces of flesh, and devouring them.

The herd continued to run for some time, but eventually slowed and went back to the site of the attack. The female was gone. Not even any bones were left. We stayed there for awhile bellowing with a low groaning sound that I had heard following the previous killing. As we moved away I felt a deep pain in my gut. Maybe it was fear and maybe it was sadness. We headed back towards the nests.

I wonder if they have been destroyed by the meat eaters too, I thought.

When we got there, the females walked around the nests looking at the eggs and moaning. They had been raided all right, very few had survived. I felt as if I had been smacked in the face. The entire herd was moaning, and I could hear myself among them.

We spent the night on that spot. My group came together that night and left the adults alone to grieve. It was nice to feel part of the group as we nestled together and slept. It was hot in spite of the rain. The night passed quickly; just before dawn we were startled awake by a roar from the herd leader. He gathered us together again and started us running.

As the morning mist lifted I realized that everyone was trying to escape the sea. It was roaring up the mountain side fast enough to keep our feet wet as we splashed upward. Blood pumped through my body in frantic thumps, and I ran like never before. After what seemed like forever, we slowed. As I looked back I saw that the immense surges of water had slowed their frantic chase. Suddenly the earth shook beneath my feet, and we were on the run again. The earth moved every once in awhile over the next few days. It was a scary, dizzying feeling, but gradually it stopped all together.

I wonder what kind of world I have come to. I thought.

We stayed on that mountain for a few days. I lost track of time, it wasn't quite so hot because of the breeze, but there was less water there too. Streams ran down to the ocean, but there were no lakes. A lot of time was spent with the teacher, whom I was calling Murray because I believed that was who he was. He would lead us into the trees and point out good and bad plants and leaves. In this spot there was something we hadn't seen before, whole fields of plants, about two feet tall and very green. Their slim stems stood straight up and grew very close together. Murray went over and tried eating a few. After a short while, he called for us to eat them too. They were delicious! They smelled nice too and reminded me of a smell I knew from somewhere else. I couldn't quite remember where. We fed on those plants for a few days, until they were so short that we couldn't eat any more; then we moved on.

CHAPTER EIGHTEEN

A Beating

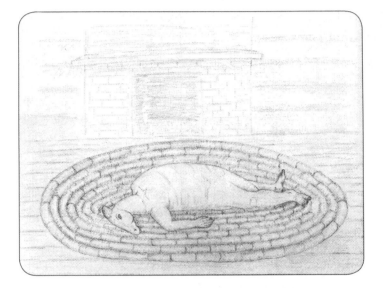

Within a few days, our leader led us back down to the sea shore. I was glad. When we saw the lakes and swamps pretty much everyone headed for the cool waters and mud. We splashed and tumbled over each other getting covered with the soothing, gooey mud. It felt so good on my sun burn and those endless bug scratches on my back and face. I swam a long time. Later the group and I rolled in the mud and splashed it onto each other, letting the relief and comfort fill our bodies. I was glad to be home.

After some rest, something terrible happened. We were in the ocean, as usual, just playing around. Suddenly a sea monster was upon us. It looked like a huge ell and had huge teeth that overlapped each other all around its long skinny jaw. Someone bellowed out the danger and we got out of the water as fast as we could, with our hearts racing. I looked around to see if everyone had made it to safety. I saw blood. My heart stopped and I just stared. It was the dinosaur that had saved me from the water monster and then become my pal.

I stood there in shock and fear. Other group members were in the water trying to help. For some reason I knew that it was too late. He had not been strong enough, yet, to help himself out of the water and up the slippery slope in time.

The howling began as the group realized what had happened. Some of them turned towards me. They walked over to me, with fire in their eyes. They kicked dirt at me and then kicked my legs. I couldn't respond. I was still too shocked. As the kicks got worse, I tried to run away, but the group circled me and wouldn't let me through. They forced me back to the middle of the circle. Now the biting started at my back and neck. I could see the blood running down my chest. I knew that I was going to die.

"Mom," I cried, but only a bellow came out of my horn. I fell to the ground.

Some time later, I woke up. As I raised my head and tried to get up, I saw Murray near by. He came over to me and bent down, nuzzling my neck. This forced me back down again. It was a relief to lie down. Everything hurt. I had no energy. Murray began licking my wounds in a long, slow movement. Inside my self I started to cry. *How can I still be alive?* I thought, but here I was.

I fell asleep again and when I woke up Murray was still there, placing some big leaves on my wounds and wetting them down. I didn't even try to get up. I felt terribly weak and sore. I slept and woke to Murray doing something to help me; I don't know how many days went by. He brought me water from his own mouth and tried to get me to eat a little. In spite of everything, I got weaker every day.

Murray kept applying those leaf bandages of his, all over the place. I drifted away again. Next time I came to, he was standing over me, gently nuzzling me. He laid something in my claw. Then he let out a long, mournful bellow, and walked away. I had a sorrowful feeling inside my body; it consumed me through and through. I knew that I would never see him again. I was sure that I would die right here, on this spot. I fell into a deep sleep.

CHAPTER NINETEEN

Going Home

There was water dripping near by. I could hear its 'ping, ping, ping' on the rocks. I was cold. I reached down and pulled the blanket higher, it felt soft and warm. The pinging was more persistent now and different, more like a bell.

Blanket? Bell? Where am I?

"I think he's waking up. Austin, can you hear me?"

I slowly opened my eyes. A dim yellow light shone above me. I turned my head toward the voice. There was a brown blur that might have been a person.

"Austin, it's me, Mom. How do you feel?"

She sounded shaky and tearful. I tried to speak, but I couldn't find any words in my head. I could feel tears running down my cheeks. I looked towards her, trying to smile.

"You're alive, thank Goodness, you're alive!" she said.

I closed my eyes and slept some more. Later I heard another voice. My vision was clearer now and I saw Dr. G. beside the bed. Mom was just behind him, with Kevin. Someone was standing over me, poking a needle into a tube.

Where was I? Where was Murray? Where is the forest?

I looked cautiously around. It's a hospital. I'm in a hospital, hooked up to a bunch of monitors and an I.V. line. That's why everyone is here. I must be pretty sick.

I looked at Mom.

"Welcome back, Austin" she smiled. Tears were streaming down her face. She bent over and hugged me. "You gave us quite a scare, young man."

"What happened?" I croaked.

"I read your note and I knew where you had gone. Austin, I am so sorry I ever made you feel so unloved. What was I thinking? I was so excited about Kevin and me that I left you out. Every day that we couldn't find you, I panicked and blamed myself for your leaving in the first place."

"I'm sorry, Mom. It was a stupid thing for me to do. I was just so depressed."

"Never again, son, please include me in all your thoughts and worries. Let's both include each other, okay. I love you."

"Thanks Mom, I love you too. Now will someone please tell me how I got here? The last thing I remember was being beaten up by dinosaurs."

"Well," said Kayla, who was standing by my bed and anxious to relate the story, "Once your Mom read your letter yesterday morning, she just couldn't stop crying and saying how it was her fault, that she hadn't been paying enough attention to you and stuff like that. We called Dr. G. right away and he and Eric were over almost before Grandma could put down the phone. What a panic."

Ryan added to the story, "Kevin and Dr. G. tried to calm her down, but was just a mess, crying one minute, scolding and angry the next. What a panic! Dr. G. explained some more about the cave and tunnels and how you could turn into a dinosaur, but that didn't help much."

I guess it didn't, Mom doesn't believe in anything magical. She must think we're all freaks and I'm the biggest one of all.

"Dr. G. said it was important to find you, to go to the cave and try to bring you back. Your Mom got really mad at Dr. G. for telling such lies."

"It was hard for me to grasp," Mom took my hand.

"I didn't want to make you feel bad, Mom. The dinosaur world is a great place."

"Well it really upset me, Austin. Your grandparents were pretty well freaked out too. They knew that something was up, but they didn't know what, until then. It really scared them."

Ryan butted in, "Your Grandpa got a search party organized with Kayla, Kevin, Eric and I searching tunnels and cave. I was really impressed with you, Eric. You didn't complain or anything. You just worked hard and long.

"Yeah, we couldn't find Austin though."

"Well that's when I got lucky," said Kayla. "A few days after you went missing I was too anxious to sleep. I got up and went to the patio to think it through. I got some juice and sat down. Bessie came over to my side and I started to stroke her. That's when the idea struck me. Bessie is a basset hound! Hounds are good at smelling things out.

I went and got her leash and one of the search lights. I threw on my old jacket and grabbed one of your dirty Tee shirts from the laundry hamper. I knew Bessie could pick up your scent. Then we were off. She was excited and tail wagging.

I hadn't expected it to be so dark and cold inside the tunnel, but I felt that I had a good chance of finding you. The search light shone down on the rocks on the tunnel floor, throwing eerie shadows on the walls and bringing the mica to life. I wished that I had woken Ryan to come with me. Even with the dog I was frightened.

In spite of that, I showed Bessie your shirt and she started wagging her tail and giving little welcome sounds. She put her nose to the ground right away and we started moving. We went a long way. My legs were tired and I was out of breath when she stopped.

"Yeah, I guess I did go pretty far in, didn't I?" I was sitting up in bed now, and paying close attention.

"Finally, Bessie stopped and looked up at the wall. She whined and wouldn't move from that spot. I moved around a bit and shone the light again. Then I saw it! Something was caught in a snag about five feet up the wall!

'Bessie, find Austin,' I cried pointing up at the crag.

She took off right away climbing that wall as if it were a stair case, when she got to the crag, she pulled something out of it and scurried down to me with it and I took your sneaker from her.

'Good dog, good dog,' I said, bolting back up the tunnel to the trap door. After that it was easy.

I woke everyone up and we got you out of there, cleaned you up and brought you to the hospital. We've been waiting three days for you to wake up.

I was sitting on the side of the bed now and wanting to get up, but Mom wouldn't let me.

"So all of you know all about dinosaur land now?"

"Yes, all the family and Dr. G and Eric know about it." said Ryan.

How can I come and go freely if everyone knows? I thought. *Then again, they almost killed me that last time, maybe this is the end of my dinosaur adventures anyway.*

"Now we have to decide what to do next."

I sat up straighter in bed, "What do you mean? I guess we just go on with our lives. Mom and I can talk things over and I don't think that I'll be going back to dinosaur land again."

CHAPTER TWENTY

A Talk with Mom

The next day I was up and walking around, checking my hospital room out, when I noticed this big egg on my night table, just as Kayla walked into my room.

"Hi," I said, "hey, do you know anything about this? It sort of looks familiar but I can't place it."

"Oh yeah," she answered, "I found that lying next to you when I discovered your body in the cave. It looked like you had been holding onto it, so I thought it might be important. That's why I kept it. Does it bring back any memories?"

"Yeah, I think so," I replied. "It reminds me of this really nice dinosaur I met when I first went there. I really don't know what to think about it. It makes me feel a bit sick to look at it, but it also makes me happy."

Dr. G and Eric arrived just after breakfast. I walked down to the lounge with them. It was a long, narrow room with a window overlooking the mountains outside. We sat where we could see the view.

"I think it will be good to get back to normal now." Dr. G. said. "We can tell the town's people the same story that we told the doctors and the police. It's very believable."

"But wait a minute, what about the town thinking that you're a murderer?" I said. "I want to talk to them about that, because I can prove the dinosaur world exists."

"Your Mom tells me that you said you don't want to go back there again," said Dr. G.

"Yes, but this is different. It's important to tell the truth and I won't have to be there for long, only until you can see my body change and then you can bring me back. There's no risk."

"Austin's right, Grandpa." added Eric, "We've already got that meeting set up with Graham and the Russells and Austin's grandparents. It should be easy to prove it to them all."

"Convince your Mom, Austin, and then get back to me," Dr. G. said, as we walked back to my room.

"Where did you get this?" Dr. G. asked as soon as he saw that egg thing on my night stand.

"Kayla said it was beside me when she found me so she brought it back in case I wanted it. I'm not sure what it is, but it must have something to do with the dinosaurs."

"I'd say it does," Dr. G. said, "Austin. This is a petrified dinosaur egg. I can't be sure, but it's likely at least seventy million years old! I can't stay right now, but we'll come back after lunch."

Mom arrived while I was eating lunch. She sat down beside my bed.

"Good, no one else is here. We can have a bit of alone time," she smiled.

"Yeah, Mom, that's great," I replied. "I like to have time with just you and me. It's been ages."

"Yes, I'm really sorry about that," she said. "I got too caught up in the moment I guess."

I picked up my sandwich and then put it down again.

"Mom, can I talk to you about something?" I asked.

"Of course you can. What is it?"

"Well, it's the dinosaur world." I said, finally taking a bite.

"Austin, you already agreed not to go back there. It is scary to even think of you ever being there even though I know it really happened."

"I know that it's scary and hard to believe, but I need you to know about what it was like. Can I tell you?"

"Of course." She picked up the fork and helped herself to some of my salad.

"It's full of wonderful smells and sights. The colors are so bright; the sky is so blue, the water is clear to the bottom, no mater how deep you go. Everything is relaxed, except when there is a crisis, and then it's horrible. I want the dinosaurs to live forever, but I know they are extinct. I think that if the dinosaurs had been smarter, they might have been able to save themselves. The thing is, we are smarter, or we're supposed to be, but we are ignoring all the warning signs about the planet. We can't even clean up a few weeds and stop polluting the air. We'll go extinct too."

"I had no idea you were worrying about such things, son. It's very complicated I think. Maybe we aren't responsible for the climate change stuff. That's what some people believe. They think it is a result of a natural shift in the climatic cycles. I think it's both. It has to do with our pollution-creating behaviors and with naturally occurring changes too."

"But Mom, there are millions of us on the earth. If each one of us could take a few steps toward cleaning up our act, that would be a big help. I never saw this as important until I went to dinosaur land. Now, I can't forget the beauty of that world and I know that we should be able to have that kind of world again. We just have to try." I took a drink of milk.

"Maybe you're right, Austin," she said, "and I'll do whatever I can to help. What do you want to do about it?"

"Well, I want to keep cleaning the beach and I want to get others to help me. I want to avoid using cars and trucks and boats and quads and all those fossil fuel users. Do you realize that fossil fuel is made from the bones of my friends, the dinosaurs? They would sure hate that."

She laughed.

"Mom, there is something else that's really important. Dr. G. has set up a meeting with Grandma and Grandpa and Graham and the Russells, right?" I asked.

"Yes, it's tomorrow night at seven, how did you know about that?"

"It's a really important meeting. He wants to tell them about his grandson Murray and how he really died. He wants to have at least a few people in this town to believe the true situation about Murray. Mom, I'm the only one that can help him out, because Murray's human body died when he was in a fight with a dinosaur, in the dinosaur world."

"Austin, don't be ridiculous!"

"I'm not, Mom, its true. He's alive, as a dinosaur and I have met him. I know it's him. I have to go back to the dinosaurs, so that people will believe Dr. G. I need to show them that it really can happen. It's safe, Mom. Dr. G. and Ryan and Kayla will pull me back if anything goes wrong. Please Mom, just talk to him about it." I blurted out my request.

"Austin, no; I can't let you do that. It's never safe and you know it. Those dinosaurs almost killed you last time you were there." She paced by the window, while she spoke.

"But Mom, this won't be like that. It will be quick, in and out again. Please just talk to Dr. G."

"What does your son want you to ask me, Ann?" asked Dr. G, as he and Eric came into the room.

"I was just telling her about the dinosaur world and how I would like to go back there once more, at your meeting on Monday night." I said.

"Ah. Well Ann?" asked Dr. G.

"He says it will be safe, but I am still hesitant to let him. How safe is it really?"

"There's never any guarantee with that sort of thing. We can see Austin's body change when he goes back and we can call him back to this side by taking the rock away from him. It should be very good odds that he'll get back in fine shape." Dr. G. replied.

"Austin, to do something like this when you're still recovering from the last time just doesn't make sense."

"Mom, I'll be out of here tomorrow and I feel fine now. Please Mom, this is really important." "We'll decide once you've been home for a few days. I'll let you know on Monday morning. Arthur, I'll want to talk to you some more before then."

I had to settle for that.

CHAPTER TWENTY-ONE

Mom's Challenge

I left the hospital the next day, which was Wednesday, and by Friday I was down at the beach again. I was only allowed to sit there and to go into the water for a bit of a cool off, no weeding today, but that was okay with me. By Monday morning I felt good, except for wondering what Mom would decide. She took me aside after lunch.

"All right, Austin, I've talked it over with Dr. G, and it seems pretty safe and also important that you do this. Tonight, you, Kayla, Ryan, your grandparents, Kevin and I will go to Dr. G's place at 7. He is inviting Graham and the Russell's and he wants Eric there too. Here's what we've decided. You'll go back to dinosaur land, but only for a very short time. If you seem to be in any trouble, Ryan will take the rock away from you and Kayla and I will call you back. Please listen carefully for us; I want you to at least be aware to listen for our voices."

"Sure Mom," I said, "You know that I can't think like myself when I'm there though, so don't expect too much."

"I know that, just keep trying to listen for my voice," she urged.

"So after tonight there will be twelve of us that know that I have been visiting the dinosaurs and seven of them will be family," I said, "I hope that will be enough people to influence the town."

"It should be."

"Okay," I said, "I'll go tell Ryan and Kayla about the plans right now." I left the room to find them.

By six forty five I had the jitters. *What should I say? How will people react when they see what happens to me? How will Mom react? She's going to freak out! I hope Kevin can help her to stay calm.*

"Let's go!" I said, trying to round everyone up. "Let's get this over with."

"Cool it Austin," said Ryan, "It's only ten minutes from here and we're just waiting for Grandma Here she comes now."

Grandma was scurrying down the hall from the kitchen, a tray of her special peanut butter/ chocolate chip cookies in her hand. We headed out. I was uncomfortable with riding in a motor vehicle of any kind, so I had persuaded everyone to walk. It was a great night, warm and still sunny. We kids ran ahead with Bessie. The adults walked and chatted. I thought they would never get there.

At the top of the drive way, we met the Russell's. The adults stopped to chat. We kids ran ahead.

"Dr. G.," I yelled as soon as I saw him, "let's do this. I want to get it over with."

"Calm down Austin," he said watching as the group slowly walking down the drive. "It looks like everyone is here now, let's go in."

We settled down on the big soft sofas in the living room. Dr. G. and Grandma laid out tea cups and pop and cookies on the coffee table. I noticed a big tub of water near by and realized it was likely for washing me off, if I needed it, after I came back from dinosaur land.

Then Dr. G. spoke.

"A few of you are here tonight because I invited you to come over to show you something amazing. This has to do with Austin's recent disappearance and injury. It also has to do with Murray's disappearance."

I noticed a questioning glance pass between Dr. Russell and Graham.

"This is so unusual that it could be called weird. I don't think that you will believe it until you see it for yourselves. After that you will have to believe it." Dr. G. said.

"Austin, are you ready?" he asked me.

"Whenever you guys are," I replied, glancing at Mom, Ryan and Kayla.

Chapter Twenty-Two

Asked to Leave

"Let's get it over with," Mom replied. She took the rock out of its bag and handed it to me.

The dizziness came and went very fast and then I was standing in the marsh. It was dusk and the water was calm. The insects had mostly settled down for the night, except for those small pests that filled the air with their low buzz and a fine black mist. The moon was huge, just about full, and the stars filled the heavens. It seemed as if they were right beside me instead of millions of miles away. There were no other dinosaurs around.

I started walking through the trees, towards the water and finally I could just make out the shapes of some kind of dinosaurs on the beach. Keeping well hidden in the trees, I walked toward them. Eventually one broke away and walked up to me. I stood still, feeling my heart pound, until I saw that it was Murray.

He stopped in front of me and when I reached him, he turned and started into the bush. I followed him. He led me back into the bushes and the marsh, where we would be hidden.

Why is he so afraid of me going to the group? I wondered. *They must still want me gone or dead?*

I could hear a noise that seemed to be coming from inside my head. What was it? We were quite close to where I had come into the dinosaur world now and the teacher seemed anxious and fretful. He was focused on a stand of tall trees, to one side. He would just look at them and then step away, then sort of creep closer again. This went on for some time. He started to growl in his throat, sounding a bit like he was hurt. Then he would move closer again.

The noise in my head sounded like a call, but I couldn't understand it. Nothing bad was happening; it was just that Murray was acting so strange.

Something bumped into me. I hit a tree trunk and almost fell over. I move over a bit, and then I felt another bump. Suddenly there was a flash of white light and I was back in Dr. G's living room. I was lying on the floor and Ryan sitting beside me and holding the stone. I could just make out what Mom was saying.

"Oh Austin, you scared me so much," she sobbed. "I called and called. Finally I had to shake you to get you to come back."

That's what the bumping was all about.

I sat up feeling dizzy. I got back into my seat on the sofa and looked around. Everyone had stunned looks on their faces. Kevin was wiping away Mom's tears and hugging her. Graham looked as if he had seen a ghost. Mr. and Mrs. Russell were holding onto each other tight, they were as white as snow!

Dr. G. broke the silence. "Alright, I know that it's hard to accept, but this is a real phenomenon. Austin can change into a dinosaur and go into the dinosaur world of the past. You saw his body start to change. You saw the horn appear on his head. You saw the distortion in his arms and legs. You saw how large his whole torso and hips became. You saw the scales and fur on his body. It is real.

Silence again.

Finally Graham spoke. "What's it feel like, Austin?" he asked.

"The first few times I did it I was really frightened. I didn't know what had happened, or where I was. It got better soon though. When I become a dinosaur I don't think like a person. I can wander around looking for good leaves or grasses, I go swimming, or for a mud bath. I stay in my group a lot, . . . or I used to." I said, feeling upset as I thought about that.

"You look a bit troubled, is something wrong with the group?" Kevin asked.

"Well they know that I am one of them, but they also can't really fit me into the daily pattern, because I come and go. On an earlier trip I had an accident and one of them had to rescue me from a water creature. That dinosaur got hurt and later he died. Since then, they attack me if I try to be with them. That's how I got so beat up last time I was there."

Mom and Grandma both gasped.

"Don't worry Mom," I said, "I don't think I'll ever go back there again. I've seen really bad stuff, like when the meat eaters kill one of the group, or eat our eggs. That's really sad."

As soon as I said it, I knew that was the wrong thing to tell her. I tried to back track.

"The best thing is the fresh air and the blue sky. You've never seen stars as bright and close as they are in dinosaur land. The water in the ocean is so clear you can see the bottom and all of the fish and stuff, even if you're really deep. The leaves taste great. There is sometimes haze in the air but only when there has been some kind of upset, like a volcanic explosion. What I notice most is the place has no pollution. Everything goes back to the earth in the end. It's great!"

"Can you feel your body change Austin?" Mom asked, wiping her red eyes, "We could see a lot of changes happening here."

"I can't feel myself change, I just get a little dizzy, Mom," I said. "When I am in dinosaur land I think that I have a real dinosaur body. I'm not Austin anymore. That's why it is pretty hard to get me to come back. If Ryan hadn't taken the stone from my hand, I don't know if I could have done it."

"But I know that you can remember it and think about the dinosaur world when you are here," Mom said, "How come you can't remember and think about here when you're there?"

"Well, I only have a dinosaur's brain when I'm there. It isn't very big."

Dr. G. broke in, "Austin isn't the only person who has ever taken trips to dinosaur land. Murray did it too and Murray died."

Graham almost choked on his tea.

"Yes, I know that I have lied to everyone about it and I know that a lot of town's people suspect that I killed him myself, but the truth is that he was fatally wounded in dinosaur land. By the time I found his human body, it was too late to save him." The room was silent. The hum of the air conditioner and the ticking of the grandfather clock seemed very loud and steady.

Dr. G. continued, "I couldn't have told you what had really happened. At that time, no one would have believed me, so I had to make up a story that would seem possible, but that didn't really work. I've been dreadfully lonely and feel guilty about it ever since, but what else could I do?"

"Can you tell us now, Arthur?" Graham asked.

Dr.G. told the whole story again. There was silence while he spoke.

I wasn't listening, I was thinking about what would happen now that more people knew about all this. *Where would it stop? Who would believe it?*

Would Dr. G. get sent to a mental home or something? What about me? What about Ryan and Kayla?

When Dr.G. stopped talking, no one spoke. Finally Mr. Russell said, "What an incredible story. It must have made things very hard for you, living with a secret like that. I never would have believed you if I hadn't seen Austin demonstrate it. I don't think you can share it with the whole town, but I'm glad that I know and can support you now."

"I agree," said Graham.

"This is a lot to take in all at once," said Dr. G. "Let's meet again over breakfast to discuss it further."

"Good idea," said Graham, "suddenly I'm exhausted."

"Let's have breakfast at our house," suggested Grandma, "I'll cook."

As we walked home, Kevin said, "I think your awareness may be useful in fighting pollution. Maybe if we do our own little bit, in our own back yard, we can make a difference.

I looked at him in amazement, "That's why I've been pulling the weeds out of the lake and all that other stuff!"

"That's a good start, Austin, How about we consider what we could do here at Shadow Lake first."

"Wow Kevin, thanks a lot," I said.

CHAPTER TWENTY-THREE

The Breakfast Meeting

Next morning, by nine, we were all gathered on the patio, over Grandma's pancakes and fresh berries from the garden.

"Try it with home made whipped cream instead of syrup," Grandma told Graham, "it's a lot better." She's right about that too.

Kevin started out by letting everyone know about our talk last night and about his idea of cleaning up just around Shadow Lake, and not the rest of the world.

"We don't have much to change here, do we? I think that the fabric of this community is defined by its remoteness and quietness," said Graham, stretching out his feet, to get more sun. "I, for one, really want it to stay that way."

"I agree, Graham," said Grandma as she passed the bacon around again, "I guess we could talk about how we can keep our town, simple and ecologically strong,"

"That's just the point, Grandma; it's not ecologically strong now." I jumped to my feet, knocking my chair over with a loud clang. "Can't you see the pollution we are causing just by allowing those huge trucks and SUVs to drive up here into this wilderness country? Can't you see how much the lake is polluted from all the boat fumes and waste that the boats dump into it. People think that it just disappears, but it doesn't, it grows. As far as I can tell, we likely compost more than city people do, but that's the only advantage we have. We're just as bad as everyone else."

I was raging mad, *my own Grand mother didn't even begin to get it.*

"Sit down Austin," said Dr. G. sternly. "We must maintain our rationality. This is the kind of talk that can get us into trouble with the town."

"That kind of talk is the only way to save our town, Dr. G." I replied sharply

"Okay, I know that this is really important to you. Now, can you tell us quietly what it is you think that you would like to do? How did the dinosaur world influence you to want to take action about pollution in this world?"

I took a deep breath. "In the land of the dinosaurs I can smell and hear and even see the real beauty of the world! It's like I think the world might be able to be if we don't pollute it so much. We could make a difference in this town and we really need to do so, before it's too late! The pollution is going to win if we don't fight back! The dinosaurs went extinct because of natural causes. They weren't able to understand what was happening and do something about it. I think that we are able to!"

"I've been thinking, about what we could do at Shadow Lake. We could restrict cars and boats and motorized water toys from the lake. We could re-stock the lake with fish, and only use row boats or canoes on the lake. That would sure change things. We could start a campaign to encourage people to buy food in plain, biodegradable wrappers, we could encourage growing vegetables. We could have a central composting place. We could plan beach cleanup days and lake clean up days too. We could make a lot of difference and what can be more important?"

"You're right, Austin," said Dr. G., "but if we challenge people so harshly or insult them, they will not listen and not cooperate."

"The whole idea is to get people to realize the damage that they are doing to the environment," I said. The patio felt hot and too full of people.

"That's your idea, Austin, it's not necessarily everyone's idea." said Dr. G. "a lot of people will want things to remain the same."

"I thought you were on my side," I yelled.

"I don't think that there are sides to this," Dr. G. replied. "We need to come up with a plan that everyone can agree to."

Grandpa was helping Grandma gather the dishes. "Getting people to change their habits is really hard work, even here at Shadow Lake. Lots of people don't believe that we are causing much pollution, or some people think that pollution is a fact of life. There are some people out there that think there is nothing that we can do about it anyway, so they don't even want to try."

"So are you all just going to give up? What were my trips to dinosaur land about anyway?

"Austin, this is the first time you have told us about your feelings regarding pollution of the environment. You tried to tell me when we took the boat out the other day, but I didn't know it meant this much to you," said Grandpa.

"It's all I ever think about any more," I replied.

CHAPTER TWENTY-FOUR

Eric

The next day, the family was all sitting on the patio having lunch when Mom told us that she had given the rock to Dr. G.

"He said that he will handle it. You will please stay away from that dinosaur dig and no more rocks. I really mean this Austin; it's very dangerous stuff you're dealing with here."

"Yes Mom. I got caught up in that other world, but I know that the group has rejected me. I won't do anything that might take me back there. What's left of the summer will be spent on the beach, I promise." I gave her a hug. "I'm sorry to put all of you all through so much worry." I said looking around at everyone there.

This family moment was interrupted suddenly by a loud banging on the back door and Dr. G. burst onto the patio. "Eric has disappeared," he said, shaking a sheet of computer paper at us. "I think he went into the dinosaur world. I can't find him anywhere. Look at this." He threw the note onto the table. "I found it just after you left, Ann."

Kevin picked it up and read it out loud.

"Dear Granddad,

I hate to do this to you, because I know that you love me, but I really want to find out if I can visit the dinosaurs. That little jerk, Austin, gets all the attention and I'm left in the mud. Not this time though. I think that I can visit the dinosaurs too! That day that I grabbed Austin's rock out of his bike carrier, I could feel the dizziness that he told us about. When I found the rock on your dresser just now, I felt it again. I want to try to go, but I don't want to come back. Life is too miserable here, but maybe the dinosaurs will accept me. Maybe Murray will be there and he'll help me fit in.

I love you a lot, but I am really upset with the people around here. They think I am just another mean city kid and maybe I am. I'm sorry about leaving, and I love you. You are my own true Grandpa and supporter in this whole world.

Eric"

We all sat there, stunned.

Finally, Grandma said, "What have you done so far, Arthur?"

"I've just had a look in the obvious places. I know Eric, and if he wants to hide himself, he will. I wanted to let you know what happened as soon as possible so I came right here."

"Okay, we need to organize a search," said Grandpa," I'll start making some calls."

"We shouldn't use local people for the search and don't call in the police yet," cautioned Dr. G., "He says he is trying to turn into a dinosaur and it sounds like he might be able to. I think he'll be in the cave, if he's anywhere."

"Yes," I said, "I think he would go there too, he already knows it will increase his chances of being able to make the change. I've got another

72

idea too; let me try. We don't know where to look for him in this world, but if he made it to the dinosaur world, I bet I know just where to find him. When I went there, I always arrived at pretty much the same spot. Sometimes I had to wander quite a bit to find the herd, but I always managed. I bet I could find him."

"Absolutely not," said Mom, "You are not going back there Austin, I don't care how much you think you could help. That's that. It's not very likely that he changed into a dinosaur anyway. Only two people have ever done it, at least as far as we know, Murray and you."

"Your Mom is right Austin," said Dr. G. "I couldn't let you do it. If something happened to you I could never forgive myself. I can't bear to lose you and Eric along with Murray." Things are hard enough as it is."

"Wait a minute," said Ryan, "Austin can go back there fairly safely if we watch him. We've always been able to judge his condition and pull him back in time. I think we should let him try."

Mom said, "No"

"Dr. G, do you remember when we were all watching him, over at your place at the very beginning of these trips." Kayla added, "We pulled him back just because he was sweating hard."

"No, No, No," cried Mom.

"Well, honey," said Kevin, with his arm around her shoulder, "If Austin could save Eric's life by taking a safely guarded trip, maybe we should consider it."

"Kevin I can't risk loosing him. What if he got caught up somehow? What if taking the rock away won't work this time?" She paused to think, we don't even have the rock, Eric has it, and it's with his human body. We couldn't even do this if we wanted to, and we don't want to." She looked triumphant.

Listening to her didn't even bother me. I was exited now. I knew how I could do it safely!

"I could go into the cave; I always get back to dinosaur land when I'm in the cave. In fact it's safer. I can see it on the walls, before I actually go there." I said, "I could maybe spot him before I even have to go into dinosaur land. If I could just go straight to him and grab him with my fore claws and mouth I could drag him back with me. All you guys would have to do is get both of us out of the cave, and then wash us down, to bring us back to reality."

"I don't think it will work like that, I think we have to be with his human body. That's where he will go back too. We've got to find it first." Ryan reminded us all.

"You're right Ryan. Let's organize that search and find that body," said Grandpa. "We'll use Bessie, just like you did, Kayla."

'Let's get going," said Kevin. He, Ryan, Kayla and Grandpa went to the other room to prepare.

"Don't involve anyone who doesn't already know about the dinosaurs," Dr. G. yelled after them.

"Don't move his body, just find it," I added as they left.

"Austin's right, Ann," Dr. G. said, "We could arrange everything that we need to bring him back, before hand. We'll get a cart to carry them out and the water and towels for washing them down can be at the mouth of the cave. We'll pre set my cell for 911, just in case."

"Why did this have to happen?" Mom cried. We all waited in silence. "All right, she finally muttered, but I want to be there every second."

"Thank you so much, Ann." said Dr. G.

"Let's go," I yelled," I was already half way to the truck.

CHAPTER TWENTY-FIVE

Back to the Cave

Dr. G. insisted that we help with all the preparations before we went into the cave. It took a bit of work, but finally everything was ready.

I spoke very little as we entered the tunnels again. It always awed me to see the beauty and glow of the tunnel walls. The sheets of crystals overhead made it feel like being underneath a sparkling waterfall. The clear blue of the stream that ran through the bottom of the tunnels, reflected off of the crystal encrusted walls.

I watched Mom as she walked beside me. She couldn't take her eyes off of the crystal formations.

"It's absolutely amazing Austin." she breathed.

Then a bit later she said, "I can see how you became enchanted by it. *She doesn't even know the half of it,* I thought.

I was loosing it. The dizziness was becoming very strong and I could see the beach and ocean on the other side of the wall now. I didn't want Mom to become upset. I started to lag behind, and I pulled Kayla back with me.

"I'm starting to see the dinosaur world. I'll change soon. Please stay with Mom, she'll freak out," I said.

"You know I will," she answered, "don't worry, just do what you have to do," and she ran to catch up with Mom.

The next thing I knew, I was in my dinosaur body. The sun blazed in a blue sky, soft with billowing clouds. I soon got my bearings as a dinosaur again. The water glistened as small waves lapped peacefully upon the sandy shore. Fish of various varieties swam around me. The air felt warm and invigorating. There were different types of trees, very tall and very lush. I felt the excitement and beauty of the dinosaur world rush up my spine and make my head tingle. Yet, in spite of the loveliness, I had a vague, uncomfortable feeling. There was something I needed to do. What was it?

I swatted at a small bird that had dive bombed in front of me, then I began to move toward the water. Something didn't feel quite right. I sniffed the air, it seemed just fine. I still had that edgy feeling; I needed to travel away from the water. I turned and started toward the forest. Why did I feel so unsettled?

Following my instincts, I wandered deeper into the forest and finally found a familiar spot.

I sniffed, yep, it smelled right, but it also filled me with fear. Where was I? As I scanned for enemies, I noticed a movement under a nearby cliff. Focusing on that spot, I stood still and watched. It was Murray. He had another dinosaur with him. Cautiously, I approached. As I got nearer I could see a second, smaller dinosaur. He was hurt. Suddenly I knew where I was. This was the place that the teacher had taken me when I had been so hurt. The teacher raised his head. He had picked up my scent. When he saw me, he made a gentle trumpeting sound through his horn. I went nearer.

The smaller dinosaur had blood on his face and neck, his breathing was labored and he was struggling to get to his feet. There was something very familiar about him. What was it?

I cautiously moved closer. Murray welcomed me with a soft rumbling in his throat, but there was nervousness about him as well. The smell of fear was strong in the air. I looked at Murray. He was looking out toward the ocean. I followed his glance. There, on the shore, was a large meat eater, his nose was in the air as he tried to locate the smell of blood. Thank goodness that their eye sight is so bad. I didn't even think about it, I just ran, at full speed out onto that beach making as much noise as possible. If that dinosaur found the injured one, it was certain death. I ran, because my life and the life of the injured dinosaur depended on it.

I was young and fast, but I hadn't stopped to notice that my enemy was young and fast too. I could hear him behind me and I could feel the earth beneath my feet vibrating with the thump of his feet. A noise started in my head, a familiar voice, but not a dinosaur at all. What was going on? I began to tire and finally knew that the enemy was catching up. At least the injured dinosaur was safe for now. I felt his breath on my rump. A flash of light and I thought, *is this it for me?*

The next thing I felt was water being splashed on my face. As soon as I realized where I was, I tried to get onto my feet. "No, not yet," I yelled, "I just found him."

I couldn't stand up in my partly dinosaur body but I could grab at the dirt with my claws. Ryan was beside me; he saw what I was trying to do and started rubbing dirt and small rocks onto my arms and legs. Finally the dizziness came.

It took me a minute to remember my location. The two dinosaurs were just where I had left them. I ran over and grabbed at the small one with my front claws, holding on tight.

The teacher stopped me with his claws, grabbing me, gently on the shoulder. He would not let go. The flash of light came and went and we were still in dinosaur world. It came again and this time I could see the tunnel and Dr. G. He was right up against the tunnel wall, looking in. What was he trying to tell me? A moment later, I felt the teacher take his hand off of my shoulder and back away. He made that small rumbling noise once again.

A final flash of light took both me and the other dinosaur back to the cave floor. For some minutes we lay there, quiet still. I was so tired. As my thoughts came back, I realized what I had been trying to do in dinosaur land.

"Where's Eric," I shouted, struggling to get to my feet. "He was with me, I had him."

"Austin, calm down," said Ryan. "They found him; he hid in the same cave that you were in. They're bringing him to us now. Let's get you cleaned up and then we'll find him."

"No, I'm fine," I lied, "Let's find Eric." I tried to move forward, but stumbled and fell. My legs were still claws, not feet at all. I looked at my hands, they were claws too.

"Are you ready to get cleaned up now?" asked Ryan.

"Yeah, I guess so," I said. He and Mom helped me out of the dig and into the tub.

Just then I saw Bessie leading the group down the tunnel. Dr. G. was pulling Eric on the tri pod thing that they had made. Kevin and Grandpa were right behind them. Eric still had a lot of dinosaur about him. He also had burns and bruises, but other than that he was all right, from what I could see.

He looked pretty rough. I had never seen myself when I first came back. It was a shock, it made me nauseated. His head was misshapen, elongated and with a horn; he had downy hair growing on his legs and paws; he was mostly a sick sort of green and in spite of all of that he still looked like Eric.

Dr G. was sitting by himself in a corner staring at the wall. He looked very intent on what he was doing, or seeing.

"What's up with him?" I asked Ryan.

"Don't know, Ryan replied, "he's been there for a few minutes, just staring like that."

I got out of the tub, dried off and got dressed, then I went over to Dr. G. and put my hand on his shoulder, "Dr. G., I'm back, Eric's back, everything is okay now," I said.

He started. "Oh, Austin, I'm so sorry, I forgot all about you for a few moments," there were tears in his eyes. "I saw Murray. I know it was him. He had Murray's eyes. I really saw him, on the wall."

"You're right, It was Murray. I'm so glad for you." I gave him a hug.

CHAPTER TWENTY-SIX

An Action Plan

Dr. G. and Mom had planned a meeting for the very next morning. We went to the castle.

Everyone was there, including Graham and the Russells. Eric was there as well. The idea was to talk over what had happened and to decide what we could do about it, if anything.

"The first thing is that I want you all to know that Eric and I have talked. We have come to some agreement as to what he will be doing in order to pay back all of you for his antics. Early this morning, I took that rock and threw it into the deepest part of the lake. At least there is now one less way to get to that horrid world of the dinosaurs."

"Eric, do you have anything to say to these people?" He said, looking at Eric sternly.

"Sorry," muttered Eric.

"I couldn't hear that," said Dr. G., "would you like to try again?"

"I'm really sorry," said Eric, much louder this time, "I don't know what I was thinking. It was a stupid thing to do and I won't ever try it again. It seemed like a great way out of my problems and it seemed like fun. Austin, I am so grateful that you came along and found me and rescued me when that meat eater came along. I'd be dead without your help. You've proved to be a real friend," Eric's jaw was quivering and his eyes were wet.

"That's okay," I told him, "I sort of got us all into this whole mess anyway."

In spite of his shakiness, when he finished speaking, he lifted his jaw and I thought I could see a bit of defiance in his eyes as he looked at his granddad.

"Alright, let's move on," said Dr. G.

"We need to decide what to tell anyone who asks about Austin's misadventure that landed him in the hospital."

Mom cleared her throat from her seat on the sofa beside Kevin,. She twisted her new engagement ring, round and round and kept her eyes on the floor. Finally she let go of Kevin's hand, lifted her head and started to talk.

"I wonder if we really need to tell the town any more about Murray and Austin. When I found out it was such a shock, that I felt like my whole world had exploded and I wanted to blow up that darn dinosaur dig. What if we tell them what Austin told you, Dad?" she said, nodding at Grandpa across the table, "We could tell anyone that asks that the stone gave Austin dreams about dinosaurs, instead of trying to convince them that the stone actually changed him into one?"

"Yeah," I said, "I've tried that a few times and it really does work. People don't even think about me actually being one. Then I could say that I was feeling depressed and ran away from home one night and was attacked by a bear. That would explain my ending up in hospital."

Grandpa agreed. "You did that when you talked to me on the boat, Austin. It worked fine. I was stunned when I really learned the truth from the note you wrote to your Mom."

There were lots of nods and uhuh's from around the room.

"What happened to that note," asked Dr. G. "I think it should be destroyed before it gets into the wrong hands."

"I tore it to bits and threw it into the fire pit," said Mom, "I just couldn't stand to have it around."

"Good. Thank you." said Dr. G.

I was thinking about everything that had happened. It seemed so long ago now.

Why are they all trying to erase my experiences? Do they want to make it seem as if it had never happened? I could feel myself getting hot and angry.

"Does everyone here agree that Austin should tell people that it's all been a dream?" asked Ryan.

"Well I'm not sure that I do." I said. "You can't make it all go away. It did happen and there are good things about it that I never want to forget."

Silence; then there was general murmuring until Kayla broke in, from across the table.

"Austin, I think you're missing the point. We don't want to make it disappear. I, for one, want to find a way that we can explain it and still let people hear about those good things that happened."

Everyone agreed.

"I think there are some steps that need to be taken," said Dr. G., I need to let the paleontology world in on the fact that there is a burial ground out here. I'll have a bit of explaining to do, but it is way past time that I made them aware. I don't think that I want to explain about the cave though. I wish it wasn't even there and then there would be no chance of them finding it."

"We could cover the entrance over before you call them," suggested Ryan, "it's very hard to see unless you're looking out for it."

"I guess that's what we will have to do," said Dr. G.

"Okay, that's settled. Now, what about the changes that I want to see happen?" I said. I pounded the table with my open hand. "We can't just ignore them. They have got to happen if we want to survive! I'm really starting to notice what I am doing to the world. Candy wrappers are lying all over the beach. Pop cans should be recycled. Washing my bike just for something to do wastes water and puts detergent into the ground. Cigarette butts and spilled pop or chips can really pollute the beach. All of those things that I was doing without thinking suddenly seem important."

"I think everyone here agrees with you Austin, but it's not necessarily a generally accepted idea," said Dr. G., "a lot of people will want things to remain the same. Lots of folks like it just the way it is."

"I thought you were on my side!" I yelled.

"Austin, I don't think that there are sides in this. We need to come up with a plan that everyone can fit into," Grandma said.

"What can be more important than saving the planet from annihilation?" I muttered.

Grandpa was listening from the kitchen. "Getting people to change because of the idea that the world may be polluting itself is hard work. Lots of people don't believe it or they think that it is happening for other reasons, such as a natural global warming cycle. There are some people out there that think there's nothing we can do about it anyway, so they don't want to bother trying."

Kevin spoke up, "Austin, lots of people feel dependant on their jobs and vehicles and instant foods and their whole way of life. They think that they are doing all they can by recycling their pop cans. It's going to be very hard to get those folks to think green in a larger way."

"So are you all just going to give up? What were my trips to dinosaur land about anyway? Maybe I should have just stayed there. It seems like I've just come back here to die anyway." I could feel my face going red again. I heard Mom gasp and I knew that I had gone too far.

"Sorry, I'm just so angry and scared." I muttered.

"Don't be," said Dr. Russell, "I think we can work something out. What would be your first line of action, Austin?"

I thought about it for a minute. "The lake and the beach; they are really dirty and the water needs to be weeded and we need to stop polluting it . . ."

"Okay," said Dr. Russell, "Let's take it one step at a time."

"I can ask the ladies of the church group to organize a beach clean up. We've done those before," said Grandma.

"That's great," said Dr. Russell, "I can approach the board of directors to petition the local government for money and equipment to clean up the lake, its long over due."

"Do you really mean it?" I said. "Wow, that's incredible," I said.

"Well then we have already taken three steps. Dr. G, you will get in touch with the paleontologists, Dr. Russell, you will talk to the board about water clean up and Grandma you'll talk to the ladies group," said Kayla.

"We can all do our part, follow up on ideas we have about this and get the word out there." Kayla added.

"Thanks you guys, you're the very best," I said.

CHAPTER TWENTY-SEVEN

The Town Helps Out

The next day we kids spent at the beach. Ryan and Kayla and Eric and I were all anxious to get started so we talked to the other kids about the ideas we had come up with. Some of them just brushed us off and went back to the water. Others were really rude. Comments like, 'Oh sure, a handful of kids can make a big difference, right?' or 'Dad says that it's just the natural way of things and we can't do anything real about it.' In spite of that, by noon we had a small brigade of ten or twelve kids talking to the picnickers and pulling water weeds. The real surprise came at supper time.

We got home and changed clothes then went out to help grandpa in the yard. He was mowing.

We got to put the clippings into the composter. We all liked the job and had done it since we were really small.

"Grandma has some good news for you, Austin." he said as I came over for my third load. "She'll tell you at dinner."

I thought it would be one of her famous desserts or something, but when we sat down to eat she said, "Austin, I talked with the ladies today and we all agree that it is time to take some environmental action in town. We will certainly have a beach clean up day. We'll start advertising it this week. We would also like to make up some posters to put up around town; they would help folks to remember what they can do to help. Things like a picture of a pop can, that said 'Recycle me please', under it or something that said 'get fit, walk or ride your bike around town, air pollution is too big a price'. It would be that kind of thing. What do you think?"

"Ryan, Kayla and I all started talking at once, "Yeah, that would be great," I said.

"Can we suggest some more ideas for the signs?" said Kayla.

"We could help make them too," said Ryan.

"That's great," said Grandma. "We'll start on them tomorrow."

Within the next few days things really started to come together. Mr. Norton, from the dump, came over. His wife had told him about the project we were starting. He wanted to help.

"I think we should really improve the dump," he said. "I've been looking at it and there is so much more recycling we could do, if we had the money. It wouldn't cost that much. We would only need a few more specialized bins and maybe two more part time people to help sort stuff. We are planning to expand anyway. I'll talk to Dr. Russell about the money."

Things were really going to get better.

Mrs. James came by. "What about a community garden? We're pretty good gardeners around here but a shared garden might provide more vegetables and fruit for the community. We could start a community farmer's market too. Last winter I had to buy strawberries in big plastic containers, shipped in from Florida. I had run out of my fresh frozen ones, from last summer."

Next time we went down to the store, Ken, the manager came over to talk to us.

"I heard from my wife about your idea. We're going to continue to use the recyclable bags of course, but we also want to stop buying things in those hard plastic containers. There are places to get them on cardboard flats. It will help a bit." We told everyone about it later that night.

"I think that encouraging composting would help too," said Grandma, "We could provide a container to every household on the lake and set up a system to arrange for pick up for anyone that didn't have a personal composting system going. All that stuff could go to the community garden."

When we rode by Mr. James place we stopped to talk. "Ever since I heard about what you kids want to do, I've been thinking about an idea." he said, "I'm really interested in cleaning up the air. All that exhaust smoke isn't good for us. We need to be using different means of transportation. I have my horse drawn wagon and I love to use it. We could restrict all motorized vehicles from the beach area to the teahouse and the restaurant. That square of land is pretty big and right now the parking is terrible. There's lots of parking just up the street in that vacant lot though. What if I ran my wagon through there on beach type days from say, ten till seven, once an hour? I could pick up people and their beach stuff; deliver them to and from the beach, or to any where else they wanted to go. I would need a helper or two, since I wouldn't be able to manage the heavy stuff and I would need a break every once in awhile. I would volunteer my time. Any one here willing to volunteer theirs?" He was looking right at me.

"I will," all three of us said at once.

"Great, thanks to all of you." said Mr. James.

CHAPTER TWENTY-EIGHT

The Egg

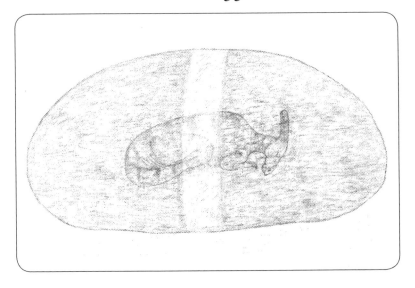

There was one more thing to do before going home. Kayla, Ryan and Eric will help me. They all have a right to do this with me. Under my bed is the egg that Murray gave to me when I got so sick. It belongs in the cave and I know it.

After dinner we kids told everyone that we were going over to say goodbye to Eric. No one questioned that. We rode our bikes over to the manor and picked up Eric. We told Dr. G. that we were just going to take one last ride around town before going home.

"Let's head up to the cave," I said, "I know of a little ledge just beyond the main part of the cave. It will be perfect for holding the egg."

"Austin, do you think that going into the cave again is such a good idea?" Kayla asked. "What if you get caught up in the dinosaur world again?"

"I'm hoping that you guys will lead me and then I can keep my eyes shut all the way, until we're just about there." I replied.

"Maybe I should stay at the entrance to act as a look out in case somebody comes by. I can play the bully and scare them off," said Eric.

"I don't think that will happen," I answered, "but we don't have to take any chances, yeah, it's a good idea."

We lowered the rope that we had stashed nearby on a previous trip and we went down, leaving Eric sitting on a rock, enjoying the view. Everything went well. Kayla was holding the egg, wrapped in its cloth because I didn't want to drop it walking with my eyes closed. I really didn't want to go into the dinosaur world. I just wanted to get that egg back to where it belonged.

As we got past the tunnel and into the cave, I could start to feel myself getting dizzy.

"Hurry, you guys," I said, "I'm having trouble focusing."

I was beginning to have that old longing to go back, just one more time. It would be so easy. Ryan and Kayla had slowed down and seemed unsure of where they were going.

"What's the matter?" I asked, "Let's go."

"It's nothing, Austin," said Ryan, "it's just so bright in here and it's getting hot too. It's not like it usually is."

My eyes opened themselves. I could instantly see the bright red light all through the cave. The walls came alive as well and I could see the dinosaurs there. They were pawing the ground and softly bellowing. Then, as I watched, the alpha male of the group trumpeted and ran up the hills and into the forest. Everyone else followed him at great speed. The sky reddened more and, as I looked, a huge ball of fire came hurtling out of the sky.

That's the comet that destroyed them, the one we studied about in school. I've got to get us out of here. I can't go to the dinosaurs ever again.

"Where's the ledge?" asked Kayla.

I glanced around and tried to stay calm. "It's over there, straight ahead then to the left," I told her, "hurry."

We were there in a few more seconds.

"This is it. I want to leave it on that little ledge." I said, pointing.

"Okay Austin," said Kayla, handing me the egg. As I went to take it out of the cloth, my hand slipped and the egg started to fall. I reached out to grab it. As soon as I touched it, I felt the change start.

No, not this time. I forced myself to concentrate. I placed the egg on the ledge, closed my eyes tightly and turned around. Kayla and Ryan each grabbed one of my hands and we all ran out. Behind me I could hear the rumbling of dinosaur feet.

They're chasing us. They were getting closer now. They seemed to surround us even as we ran. I could hardly keep my balance because of the shaking and the dust was so thick. It was hard to breath.

"Do you feel that?" asked Ryan, coughing.

How can Ryan be hearing the dinosaurs? How could the dinosaurs be following us? They have never come into our world before.

I looked back quickly. The cave was full of dust and smoke and the walls were trembling, but there was no sign of any dinosaurs.

What is going on?

Suddenly I knew. It wasn't dinosaurs chasing us. It was an earthquake. We had to get out of there and fast!

We raced for the end of the tunnel. We could hear Eric yelling for us from above.

"Grab the rope, quickly, we have no time, hurry," he said.

Ryan and Kayla pushed me ahead so I had to climb out first. I started to climb and Eric tugged. Finally I was at the top. We sent the rope back down and soon Kayla was standing beside us. We needed one final attempt for Ryan. Before he could get half way up, the earth increased it's shaking. We kept on pulling. He made it. He was badly bruised from banging against wall, but he was okay.

"Run," Eric cried. "We need to move or we'll be buried."

We sped through the forest, away from the tunnels. Finally we stopped to catch our breath. The shaking had stopped . . . for now.

"Wow, said Eric, thank goodness we all got out."

"Yeah, and I got the egg in the right place too."

"That's good." Kayla replied.

"I wondered what happened at the tunnel entrance, do you think we could go back and take a quick look?" Ryan asked.

"Yeah, lets," I said.

We walked slowly back to the edge of the clearing. There was dust everywhere. At first I didn't even recognize it as the right place. Rocks were still rolling down the hill. Then Ryan saw the rope lying in the rubble.

"This is it, I guess, or at least what's left of it," he said.

"Yeah, you're right, there's no sign of the entrance way now. At least we don't have to fill it in," I said.

"Let's get out of here," said Eric.

We walked away. My heart had stopped racing and I was breathing naturally again. I thought about that egg.

"How did it go?" asked Eric.

"Fine," I said, "It's done. Do you think we can go back to normal life again?"

"It will never again be the same for any of us," he said quietly.

"Thank goodness," said Kayla. "I have had enough excitement for one summer."

"Well I know a couple of things for sure. Life in this town will be healthier and safer now and we've had the greatest adventure possible. Maybe normal will be okay, at least for awhile."

"Yeah," said Ryan, "I'm all for that.

CHAPTER TWENTY-NINE

An E-mail from Grandma

Hi to all of our grand kids:

How are you all doing now that you are back in school and into a weekly routine again? I guess it's very different from the summer you just had.

I'm writing to let you know everything that has happened since you left. We have been very busy here. The church ladies have been making posters like mad and they have adopted a dinosaur theme. Each poster has a dinosaur on it, watching someone do something that will help lessen the pollution. They are all smiling of course. They are everywhere. Down at the dock one says "Fun doesn't need fuel." Another one, at the store, says "If you can't recycle it, do you really need it?" I won't tell you any more, you'll see for yourselves when you come back next year.

We had the first beach clean up day a few days ago. Lots of people came out to help and we all pitched in. We walked and picked up stuff and noticed how bad it really was. I picked up lots of cigarette butts and nails and sharp bits of rusted cans. The other thing was that we got to talk to people. It was surprising how many people really want to get involved and think the ideas we have so far are great. I sure hope the enthusiasm lasts. Another clean up day is already planned for the spring. Folks are planning a farmer's market and a community garden for next summer. It is hoped that we can sell fresh fruit and vegetables to the tourists. Mr. Reed and Mr. Barnes have donated a site for the new community garden; it will start up in the spring. Lots of the men have offered to help get it going.

The biggest news is that Dr. Russell has gotten the government to fund a clean up of the lake. That is now scheduled to take place in the spring as well. In the meantime, some of the people who support our ideas got together and formed a committee. They called it the Environmental Considerations Committee. So far it has come up with these new ideas. They want to put some of the old tires that have been collecting at the dump onto a special area of the beach. It seems that geese love to use tires as nesting sites, so this would draw them to one spot rather than have them all over the beach like they are now. Mr. Randall, you know him, he's the water equipment rental man, has agreed to bring in ten canoes and ten rowboats for this summer. They will be an alternative to the motorized vehicles. We have a new sign on the dock. It reads, 'Fun at the beach does not require motorized vehicles.' It will be interesting to see how that turns out.

The district has agreed to supply us with small, household composting containers for everyone in the community. They should arrive before summer does. Mr. James will get paid by the district to collect the containers once a week and he will use them to compost the community garden. He has spent all of August giving everyone horse and buggy rides through the main part of town. People just love the idea and he gives a running commentary of the benefits of this type of travel.

Mrs. MacKay has even taught all of the ladies how to knit nice purses out of old plastic bags! The Bradfords, who sell the solar panel units up here, have agreed to have a half price sale all next summer, on any solar panels that people buy. Things are changing, thanks to you kids.

I hope you each have a great Christmas and, as always, we look forward to seeing you next year.

We Send Lots of Love, Grandma and Grandpa.

THE END